Like Mother, Like Daughter?

14 stories about girls and their mums

Selected by

Bel Mooney

KINGFISHER

For my Kitty
and all daughters – B.M.

KINGFISHER
An imprint of Kingfisher Publications Plc
New Penderel House, 283-288 High Holborn
London WC1V 7HZ
www.kingfisherpub.com

First published by Kingfisher 2006
2 4 6 8 10 9 7 5 3 1

This selection and introduction copyright © Bel Mooney 2006
Cover illustration copyright © Eliz Hüseyin 2006
The acknowledgements on page 256 constitute
an extension of this copyright page

The moral right of the compiler, authors and illustrator has been asserted.

All rights reserved. No part of this publication may be
reproduced, stored in a retrieval system or transmitted
by any means electronic, mechanical, photocopying or
otherwise, without the prior permission of the publisher.

A CIP catalogue record for this
book is available from the British Library.

ISBN-13: 978 0 7534 1146 9
ISBN-10: 0 7534 1146 6

Printed in India
1TR/1105/THOM/SGCH/80GSMSTORA/C

Contents

Introduction

When you think of it, the mother-daughter relationship is the most important one there is. Yes, of course I hear it for fathers and sons! But the bond between two women, that link between the generations, is such a special mix of contradictions. It can be hard at times – especially when the daughter is trying to spread her wings, whilst Mum wants to keep her tied to the nest a bit longer. When it's good, mothers and daughters can be the greatest of friends. And when it's bad… just run for cover.

The title of this wonderful collection of stories can be read in different ways. I think "like mother… " can sound like an instruction – or a plea. Try to like your mother, even when she is irritating, and she will cling to liking you, during the years of teenage tantrums! Love each other, yes – but like each other as well, so that you treat each other as people, not just family. That's where the chance of friendship lies.

Then there are the words that sing through our veins, the old refrain of the genes: "You're like me, and you can't help it." I've often heard a friend say that when she grew up she realised she was starting to sound "just like Mum". We mothers pass on our little ways, and the daughter who moans about them will find herself picking them up just the same. But we learn from our daughters too – about what not to wear, about the latest sounds, even useful slang. Influence passes both ways.

As a mother myself, I think of my daughter Kitty (the inspiration for all my children's books) as a kind of messenger sent by me towards the future, to do what I hoped, and what she thought I hoped, as well as what she truly wants. Is it any wonder she has become a journalist, just like me? We've had our share of quarrels, and more than our share of fun. The truth is, I can't help thinking of her as a mini-me, especially when she's at her best. And when she's not? Oh, please – that's her dad's side!

Of course, I am a daughter too. I know what I owe my own mother, but also realise that I have done things she couldn't have dreamt of – for her or for me. Not that we sit around talking about it. Life's too short – and anyway, we just like to go shopping. And she loves to take Kitty shopping too, flattered when people think she's Mum, not Gran. And so it goes on: the strong yet fragile daisy-chain of female relationships.

I asked writers in Britain and the United States to come up with stories on this theme, knowing they would feel inspired. More than one wrote back saying she had been both a daughter and a mother, so the problem would be what not to write! Worried we would have too many cosy tales, I should have known better. When I gave my own daughter one of these stories to read (I won't say which one), though grown up now, she got tears in her eyes and said, "Mum, I can't bear it." That's the trouble. Real life – in all its complications – often feels unbearable. But sometimes books can help.

When I go to schools to talk to younger children about my own books, there's a word I usually have to explain. It's "universal". I tell them that although some of us are rich and some poor, some living in big houses, some in tiny flats, some living with both parents, some adopted or living with relatives, however we live, we all wish for things. We all get sad sometimes, and we all lose stuff, and we all feel disappointment, and (with luck) we all love. That's what universal means. Big things we share.

So all over the world, the ups and downs of family relationships are similar, no matter what language is used for those quarrels. Because you can be sure of this: in a tribal village or a mighty city, right now, there is a girl thinking her mother doesn't understand her, and a mother wishing her beloved girl wouldn't be so mean. There's a mother-daughter team making up and linking arms and walking out to the shops to buy new clothes, as though they were going out to conquer the world. And others are wandering down to the village market, to buy food for the meal they will make together. And others sitting down to whisper about husbands and boyfriends...

I hope you'll read this collection and understand a bit more about your own relationships. Mothers and daughters can share the book, and laugh, and cry – and then look at each other and say, "I told you so!" Because that's how it is.

Bel Mooney

Tantie

ADÈLE GERAS

"Why," asked Lorna "is our family, like, so odd?"

"There's nothing odd about it," Tantie answered. "Not that I can see. Whatever do you mean?"

Lorna and Tantie were on their way to visit Gran, who was Tantie's mother, in the Roseview Home. This took about twenty minutes by bus, which gave them a good chance to chat. Tantie was easy to talk to.

"Well, your name for a start. No one calls their aunt 'Tantie'."

"They might if they had an auntie called Tanya. Tanya and Auntie… Tantie. Rhyming with scanty and panty, don't forget!" Tantie giggled. She often giggled, which was one of the things about her which was odd. No one else's aunt, as far as Lorna could see, ever did that. They laughed but they didn't giggle.

"I think it's because you're not very old," Lorna said. "You're only twenty-nine."

"Nearly thirty. No spring chicken," said Tantie.

"But you dress…well…"

"Not like the other mums. But that's one of the advantages to being an aunt, don't you see? Aunts are famously eccentric."

Tantie ran her hands through her bright red hair and pushed her enormous glasses further up her nose. The frames were red, to match her hair. She was wearing black-and-white patterned tights under a denim skirt and had a pink feather boa wound round her neck.

"You look like a teenager," Lorna said. "And anyway it's not just that… there are no men in our family. None at all. That's… well, that's unusual."

Tantie sighed. "It's just worked out like that. It's not deliberate. We like men. Your mum was married … to your dad."

"But he's gone, hasn't he? According to Mum, he disappeared not long after I arrived. He must have hated me. Maybe it's my fault there are no men about."

"Don't be silly, Lorna. Nothing to do with you. Anyway, we're here now."

She bounded down the steps from the top deck of the bus and Lorna had the distinct impression that her aunt was glad the conversation had come to an end for the moment. Lorna wasn't. She wasn't so keen on visiting Roseview these days.

Gran had been in the home for seven years, and

was very lucky to have got a place, according to Mum. It was only because Mum was the matron's secretary that Gran was allowed to be there. Normally, Mum said, a room at Roseview cost the same as one in a five-star hotel.

"Why does Gran have to live there?" Lorna used to ask when she was much younger. She couldn't understand what was wrong with their house, which was actually Gran's house. That was quite big enough for the four of them. It turned out that Gran was becoming forgetful and it was, Tantie said, kinder to her to put her somewhere where she could be with other people, who could remind her of things.

"And, don't forget," Tantie added, "she's got her own daughter there every day, hasn't she?"

Perhaps it was more sensible to keep Gran safe, but somehow Lorna still felt her proper place was in the kitchen at home, cooking tea for everyone, or leaning against the sink with her apron on and a big smile on her face.

Lorna used to look forward to visiting Roseview. When she was five, she loved going to see her gran. All the other old ladies in the communal lounge had fussed over her, and given her sweeties, and listened to her sing nursery rhymes that she'd learned at school. Gran was proud of her, too, and that felt good. In a loud voice, she used to tell everyone: "This is Lorna, my daughter Becky's daughter. Isn't she a pet? Becky's Matron's secretary…" As if they needed reminding. It struck Lorna that old people were funny like that: they didn't seem to mind a bit being told things over and over again. They liked it, and kept nodding their heads, and putting out their hands to touch her and admire whatever she was wearing.

She and Tantie went up the front steps and in through the big doors, then along a passage with a very shiny polished floor to Mum's room.

"Hello, Becky! We're here!" said Tantie, sticking her head round the door.

"Hello, Mum," said Lorna. "Is Gran in the sunporch?"

"Yes, dear," said Mum. "She's expecting you." She smiled briefly and then bent her head to look at her work again.

Lorna felt guilty. She felt guilty whenever she thought properly about her mum. It wasn't that she didn't love her. Of course she did. Mum was kind, and efficient, and wore proper clothes: suits and high-heeled shoes. She saw to it that everything at home worked properly, though Tantie did the cooking (in her way, which she called "inspired" and Mum called "erratic"). Somehow, she never seemed to have any time to do the things Lorna wanted to do. Once, not long ago, Lorna had plucked up the courage to ask her about it.

"We never do stuff together, Mum," she said.

"Of course we do," Mum answered. "What sort of stuff do you mean?"

"Well… go shopping. Go to the movies. Go for walks… you know."

Mum had blushed and Lorna immediately felt bad. "I'm sorry, dear. I do have my job and then at the weekend there's the cleaning and laundry and so forth… it's not easy. And anyway, Tantie likes that sort of thing much more than I do. You've got her too, you know."

Lorna nodded. "Yes," she said. "Tantie's good fun."

"There you are then, you're lucky. Best of both worlds."

Lorna could never, ever say what she really felt, though, which was that she loved Tantie much more than she loved her own mother. Even thinking such a thing made her feel terrible. You weren't supposed to love anyone more than your mum. No one. Mums were special and wonderful and you made Mother's-Day cards for them at school and bought them flowers and everyone said they were the most important influence on how you were, what your character was and what you became when you grew up. If someone became a criminal, everyone said *What were his parents thinking?* but they meant the mum, usually. When people got divorced, the kids went with the mums, more often than not. Lorna had asked all her friends who they loved best in the whole world and every single one of them said their mum and dad. As she didn't have a dad, she didn't have the option of loving him best, so it distressed her that the person she loved best was her auntie.

"Come on, Lorna, you're daydreaming again," said Tantie. They were in the lounge now. You had to go through that to get to the sunporch. Some old ladies were sitting in armchairs pushed right back against the walls. Lorna and Tantie knew a lot of them, because they were Gran's friends, so they had to stop and say hello. Lorna looked down at the beige and pink and green flowery carpet, because she didn't like to see the faces covered with wrinkles and brown spots, or the hands, which looked a bit like old tree roots.

Gran was all by herself in the sunporch. She looked just the same from the back, but Lorna knew that, from the front, her bright blue eyes were faded, and she didn't smile nearly as much as she used to. Lorna dutifully kissed her, and then sat on a chair while Tantie gave her the grapes they'd brought and put the magazines she liked reading on a small table next to Gran's chair.

"Lorna… is it Lorna?" Gran said, peering at her grandchild. "Come and tell me what you've been getting up to, darling."

It was hard to know how to tell Gran things, because you were never sure that she understood what you said. Nevertheless, Lorna went through a list of the things they'd done at school. She had just started to speak about the display they were going to do at her ballet class, when Gran interrupted and spoke to Tantie.

"She's getting more and more like you, you know."

"Lorna? Nonsense. She looks like her dad, Mother. We've always said so."

"No, she doesn't. Spit and image of you, Tanya. I'm good at resemblances, me."

Tantie raised her eyebrows at Lorna and made a funny face, as if to say *Gran's lost her marbles.*

"Are they taking you all to the pantomime this year, Mother?" Tantie turned the talk away from who looked like whom and Lorna was grateful. She hated people discussing her. She half-listened as the talk drifted about in the warm afternoon and thought about what Gran had said. Did she really look like Tantie? It was possible, Lorna supposed, that she did. Tantie looked nothing like Mum, even though they were sisters. Maybe the resemblance had taken a kind of side-step. Tantie looked more like Gran than Mum did, so maybe Lorna looked like Gran. She sighed. It was getting a bit boring, just sitting here, and she began to wish they could go home.

❦ ❦ ❦

Lorna and Julie were playing "Pop Idol" in Lorna's bedroom.

"We need jewellery," said Julie. "And some eyeshadow. Hasn't your mum got some things we could borrow?"

"She's at work. And anyway, she doesn't have anything we'd like. My aunt, she's the one with the bling."

"Ask her, then. She's downstairs, isn't she?"

Lorna ran down and Tantie, because she was busy making pizza dough from scratch ("No packet mixes for me!") waved her away with a vague, "OK, but put everything back, please."

"Your aunt," Julie said when Lorna came back with Tantie's things "is better than Topshop."

The girls draped themselves with beads and scarves and put coloured eyeshadow on their eyelids and danced about to music from the CD player. When Julie went home, Lorna took all the borrowed finery and went downstairs to put it away.

The house was very quiet. That meant that Tantie was out. Mum was in the front room, on the sofa, reading the newspaper and probably snoozing over it. She often did that, which she said was a sign of age, even though she wasn't that old. She was twenty-four when Lorna was born, which made her thirty-six now. Mum said Tantie was not much better than a teenager. She usually said it in a sniffy way when Tantie had done something mad, like dyeing the curtains bright yellow.

Tantie's bedroom was Lorna's favourite room in the whole house. Her bed was heaped with satin and velvet covered cushions, she had lots of interesting-looking books in a tall bookcase and framed pictures of friends and family all over one wall. Lorna liked the ones of herself as a baby. Every time she looked at one carefully, she thought, *I was dead cute.* The best picture of all showed baby Lorna sitting on Tantie's lap on the sofa in the front room (a different sofa but the same room). Next to Tantie sat a very good-looking young man.

"Who's that?" Lorna had asked, years ago. She remembered the whole conversation.

"His name was Danny," Tantie had told her. "My boyfriend at the time. When you were a baby."

"He looks really nice. What happened to him? Why didn't you marry him?"

"I would have, only he scarpered. Joined the Navy and disappeared. Never saw him again, after that."

It was obvious that Tantie couldn't really have loved Danny, or she would have made more effort to keep him. When Lorna had asked why there were no photos of her dad, Tantie said that he was "camera-shy" and added: "Besides, he wasn't here long enough to have his picture taken."

Lorna pulled open the bottom drawer of the chest of drawers and started to put the scarves back. Her hand caught the drawer-liner as she did so, and she caught sight of a brown something... She leaned over. It looked a bit like a letter: one of those envelopes that school reports came in.

Lorna pulled it out and turned it over in her hands. There was a piece of paper inside. She held the envelope up to the light and couldn't see anything. Suddenly, she knew she was going to do something she wasn't supposed to do. She was going to open the envelope and see what was inside. Or was she? For a moment she hesitated. You were definitely not supposed to read other people's letters. Mum and Gran and even Tantie had made sure she knew that. But what if you could do it safely? What if no one ever found out you'd done it? Then it would be OK, because it would be as though you'd never done it... and anyway, maybe it wasn't a letter. Maybe it was a cutting or something. From a newspaper.

When she saw what was in the envelope, she almost put it straight back. It was a certificate, very official-looking and printed in red. Then her own name caught her eye.

Lorna Mary Bradshaw
Born 19th May, 1993

Yes, that was her birthday. This was her birth certificate. It must be.

Mother:
Tanya Susan Wallace
Born 20th July, 1976

Father:
Peter Summers
Born 6th September, 1975

Lorna blinked. She read it all over again. Mother… Tanya Susan. That was Tantie. Her second name was Susan. That was her birthday. July 20th. Gran was always going on about how hot it had been when she was having Tantie. What did this mean? Could it… was it?

"There you are, Lorna. Coming to have pizza? I've been slaving away… what's that?"

Lorna held up the certificate for Tantie to see. "I don't understand this," she said. "Does it mean… But how could it?"

Tantie sighed and sat down on the bed. "Come here, Lorna. I have to tell you something… I did hope that I could get away with it, but actually, I'm glad you found that. You look as though you've been turned into a statue. Come and sit down. Next to me. After all, I'm your mother, as you've discovered by accident. I'm so sorry, darling. I never, never meant you to find out like this…"

Lorna sat down next to Tantie. She shook her head. "I don't understand anything. Why is Mum… I mean, why did you…?"

"I was very young. I was sixteen. I wasn't old enough to be a mum."

"What about Mum? What did she… I mean…"

"She was married. It made sense. I couldn't have given you up for adoption. Have you any idea how much I love you? Your mum… she saved me. She's been so good to us, Lorna. She wouldn't hear of giving you up. That's why your dad left… I mean Becky's husband of course. He thought she was mad. To help me out, I mean. And somehow, there never has been anyone else, since. Not really. But we've been happy here, haven't we, Lorna? You've never felt the lack of a mother, have you? That's because you've had two… two mothers."

Lorna nodded. "Were you ever going to tell me? Did you ever discuss it? You and Mum? And anyway, why couldn't you have been the mother? Lots of people have babies without being married, don't they?"

"Yes, they do, but I was still doing my A-levels. Mum and Gran both said I had to go on to university. I wanted to go, too. I was glad I went."

"Didn't you miss me?"

"Yes, I did, but it was only three years. And I came back every holiday, to see you. I had to allow your mum to bond with you, too. It was only fair to give her the chance… to be a proper mother. It was the least I could do for her, after all she'd done for me."

"But what about my dad?" Lorna asked.

"He never knew about you. He'd gone long before you were born. And I never told Danny the truth. Perhaps I should have done."

Lorna briefly considered what it would be like to have such a handsome father. She couldn't imagine it.

Tantie stood up. "There you are, love. Life is more like a soap opera than you think. Everyone's life, not just ours. We'd better go down and tell your mum what's happened. Over pizza."

"You're my mum."

"I suppose I am. But I'm your Tantie too. Sometimes I think it's better to be a Tantie."

Lorna said nothing as she followed her aunt… her mother… downstairs. At least she no longer needed to feel guilty about loving Tantie more than she loved Mum. *I was right all along. I did love my mum best.* She remembered what Gran had said about how she looked like Tantie, and glanced in the mirror as she left the room. *I'm going to be just like her when I grow up,* she thought, and ran down the stairs to the kitchen.

Becoming an MPG

CANDICE RANSOM

Reigning MPG, Brittany Holmes, saw me reading a poster in the cafeteria this morning. The poster announced the eighth-grade dance a week from today.

Brittany swished over to me, musky waves of Ambush perfume trailing in her wake. She had the same heavy-lidded confidence of the girl in Josh Campbell's new music video, "Don't Look Back".

"You aren't thinking of going, are you, Kendra? I mean, I've never seen you at a dance." She thrust one model-thin hip forward and waited for my answer.

I hadn't any intention of going to the dance. By now, I was resigned to my position on the bottom of the popularity heap, where I'd spent my entire life, thanks to the MPGs.

I first encountered an MPG when I was five. Every school has them, even in kindergarten. Mean Popular Girl. MPG for short. They're the ones who say who's cool and who's not.

My mother had made my first-day-of-school

dress. It was yellow, with Scottie dogs on the pockets. I twirled at the bus stop and my skirt fluttered. I couldn't wait to begin kindergarten.

But then I met Summer Philips, who had hair so long she could sit on it. Summer was the envy of the other girls, including me. She wore a pink party dress with glittery buttons and looked like a princess. The boys chased her more than any of the other girls in the playground.

Summer came up to me and said, "Your dress is ugly and stupid. Mine is prettier." I looked down at my stupid Scottie-dog pockets and wished I had pink, glittery buttons. I no longer felt like twirling.

Between my scraggly hair and The Ugliest Dress in the World, it was all over for me. At Circle Time, Summer relegated me to the edge of the rug, where the boys wiped their snot. Summer and her friends sat comfortably on the fluffy part of the rug.

Throughout elementary school, the MPGs ruled with an iron crayon. If you didn't have what they said was cool, or didn't wear what they wore, you paid the price by being sent to the snot seat, or its equivalent.

So when Brittany Holmes asked if I was going to the dance, as if that was the most outrageous notion she'd ever heard, something inside me snapped. It had been a long time coming. I was tired of the snot seat, tired of being unpopular and invisible. It wasn't that

I liked Brittany Holmes. But I envied her golden throne. If I became an MPG, my life would sparkle like Summer Philips's buttons.

"Just as I thought." Brittany gave me that braces-half-smile that always made her look smug. "You aren't going."

Before I could catch them, the words tumbled out of my mouth. "Actually, I am." I turned on my heel, tossing over my shoulder, "See you there!"

My knees felt weak as I headed for class, but my blood zinged with excitement. I could do this! With the right clothes, I could become an MPG!

Next Friday, I'd walk into the gym, pause dramatically in the doorway so Brittany and her cronies could get a load of me, and then I'd dance and laugh and have a great time. They'd see what a cool person I was and initiate me into the privileged world of the MPG.

All I had to do was convince my mother that if I didn't have an outfit exactly like other girls would be wearing, I had no reason to go on living.

I sat beside my mother in our old Ford Explorer as we drove through our neighbourhood. Daddy lived in the next state in a brand-new apartment complex with a pool and a fitness centre and hiking trails. It was nice, but I preferred my older neighbourhood, where little kids pedalled tricycles

LIKE MOTHER, LIKE DAUGHTER?

and dogs barked from behind white fences.

"How was school?" Mom asked.

"Got a B on my maths test."

"Great! And you thought you'd fail it."

Friday night was errand night. When Mom got home from her secretarial job, we always went to the mall. After Mom and Daddy divorced three years ago, Mom said, "Instead of ordering in pizza and watching a video like we used to, let's go out on Fridays. Make it a girls' night. Just you and me."

Picking up the dry-cleaning or buying groceries wasn't boring when my mother and I carried on like best friends. Mom had a wicked sense of humour. When Daddy started dating Jennifer, Mom joked, "I'm glad he found a college student to pick up his socks. She probably has a lot more energy than I did."

We sort of hated Jennifer together until I went to stay with Daddy last summer. I met Jennifer and liked her. She was a lot of fun. And she bought me one of those Italian add-a-charm bracelets that everyone was wearing.

"Did your father get you that?" Mom asked when she picked me up.

"Jennifer," I said. "She's really not so bad, Mom." Mom didn't say anything. After that we never mentioned Jennifer's name again.

Now I looked over at my mother. She was

massaging her neck with the hand that wasn't on the steering wheel. "Hard day?" I asked.

"Brutal. Thought I'd never finish that early-education policy report that's due on Monday. Mr Pittman was making changes right up to going-home time."

"I'll give you a back rub when we get home."

She smiled over at me. "What would I do without my girl?" With a sigh, she added, "Thank goodness it's Friday! Where shall we eat? Banjo's?"

"Sounds good."

We fell silent then as night drew around us. It was only a fifteen-minute drive to the mall, but I couldn't wait to get there. I wondered why it is the trip seems longer when you are going someplace than coming home. I hummed my favourite Josh Campbell song, "Don't Look Back".

Mom wore her errand-night jeans and sweatshirt, her worn leather handbag resting on the seat between us. At traffic lights, she absently zipped and unzipped the flap, a thick, zuck-zuck sound I found oddly pleasant. Our Friday-night ritual made me feel warm inside, as comforting as a cup of cocoa.

But this Friday the routine was going to be different.

We drove down Lee Highway and turned off onto Route 28. As we approached the top of the long hill, I watched for the first glimpse of the distant Blue Ridge mountains. Purple with dusk, the mountains marched north to south in an unbroken chain, like a parade of elephants. Seeing them always made me feel exhilarated, as if I was on the verge of discovering something important.

The night was so dark, it seemed as if my mother and I were the last people on earth. The black road spooled ahead of us, edged with trees and telephone poles. When we rattled over the bridge spanning the Bull Run river, I crossed my fingers, something I'd done since I was a kid, afraid we wouldn't make it to the other side. A few lights shone through the windows of houses we passed, and sometimes the ghostly blue glare of a TV. I imagined families inside, watching a programme together, and felt a little lonely.

After so much unrelieved darkness, the mall burst upon us in a festival of lights, like Fourth of July fireworks. Mom pulled into a space in the corner of the car park. In my excitement, I jumped out of the car before it stopped rolling.

"Kendra!" Mom yelled. "Get back here!"

I realised this was no way to launch my plan and meekly swallowed the telling-off she gave me. Our first stop was the bank. Then we went to the Price Club and stocked up on thrilling items like toilet paper and light bulbs. After we carried the stuff to the car, we went into the mall to the best department store.

"I'm only here for underwear," Mom said. "There's a lingerie sale this week."

My heart tripped to a new rhythm. Win-tonight. Win-tonight.

Mission MPG had officially begun.

I saw the outfit in the Junior section of the shop straightaway. A mannequin modelled a pink scarf top and low-slung jeans split all the way up the sides. The slits were laced with leather. The MPGs had already set the fashion barometer at Frost Middle School by wearing low-slung jeans and scarf tops. The other girls were copying them fast.

My mother was heading to the underwear department, giving me about three seconds to nail her attention.

"Mom!" I shrieked. "Look! Isn't that the cutest outfit you've ever seen? See it? Oh, Mom, I just love it! Can I have it? Can I, can I, please?"

She stopped in her tracks and turned around to stare at me as if she'd never seen me before. Maybe she wished she hadn't. At least half the people in the shop were gawking at us. Begging on errand night — or any night, for that matter — was strictly forbidden. If I wanted something, I was supposed to ask for it in a reasonable tone, and if I couldn't have it, that would be the end of it. Full stop.

But tonight I had too much at stake to follow the rules. I knew my mother's arguments if I asked reasonably for a new outfit. "I didn't come into this shop to buy you clothes, Kendra," or "We don't have the money." She always said stuff like that, which was why I had to resort to drastic measures and catch her off guard.

"What?" she said in a dazed voice.

"This outfit, I have to have it!" I pointed at the mannequin like somebody who had gone berserk. "The back-to-school dance is next Friday and I want to go. Will you buy this for me to wear, Mom, please, please? Pretty-please with sugar on it?"

"Kendra, for heaven's sake, you know we don't have the money for clothes tonight."

"You always say that! We never have enough money for anything," I wailed. "Everybody gets new things but me! I wear the same old rags, day in and day out."

I hadn't whined since I was five years old. But for a shot at the lofty throne of an MPG, I'd stoop as low as I had to.

Now my mother tugged the price tags into view, then crammed them back, her lips in a thin line. "We simply can't afford this, Kendra. I'm sorry."

I wasn't giving up that easily. "Then buy it for me

for Christmas! I won't ask for another thing, I promise!"

"I've already bought your Christmas present. Back in July when it was on sale – "

"Take it back! Whatever it is, I don't want it. I want this!" I hurled myself at the mannequin's feet, nearly chipping a front tooth on its shinbone.

My mother was mortified. "Get up this instant!" she said. When I stood up, my face suitably tear-streaked, she sighed and examined the jeans. "First of all, these jeans are for a girl much older than you. You're not leaving my house in trousers split right up the leg."

I had had a feeling she'd say that, and was ready with Plan B. I quickly pulled a pair of silver-studded jeans from the next rack. They were just as cool. "How about these, then?"

After examining the jeans to make sure they were decent, she said, "It's more than I budgeted for Christmas, but I suppose you can have another present."

"I don't have to wait till Christmas to wear them, do I?" I asked, panic welling in my throat. Sometimes my mother laid down conditions.

"No. But I don't want you to conveniently forget about them and ask for something else later." She took the hanger from me. "OK. Let's go."

"Wait! What about the top?" I pointed to the scarf top on the mannequin.

She shook her head. "Too expensive. Wear your blue T-shirt."

"I don't want to wear my blue T-shirt! I want a scarf top!" My voice escalated to a shrill note that could only be heard by dogs.

My mother peered at me. "Are you feeling OK? You're acting like a two-year-old."

"I'll be fine once I have a scarf top."

"Kendra, I'm not made of money." She tapped her foot impatiently.

"But, Mom, everyone has a scarf top." All this begging was giving me a headache, but I had to persevere. I was almost there.

"And why do you have to have that exact top?"

I stared at her. Did she honestly think I'd ever be anybody at school if I didn't look like everyone else? "Forget it. I'll just stay at home next Friday and do my maths homework... or maybe some extra work to impress my teachers – "

She studied the top from all angles. "I can make you one a lot cheaper."

"Will it be pink?"

"I have some green print fabric at home. It'll do."

I remembered that weird material. "Can't we buy some new material?"

"If you want a top like this, it'll have to be green." Her tone said I had pushed her as far as she was going.

I conceded the point. A weird green scarf top was better than none.

"OK," Mom said, after paying for the jeans. "Let's go."

Naturally she wanted to get out of the shop as quickly as possible, but her route took us right past the cosmetic and perfume counter. We practically walked into a towering display of Ambush. The MPGs wore so much Ambush, a perfume cloud surrounded them like fog.

I gazed longingly at those ruby glass bottles. I had the right clothes. I'd really be in if I had the right perfume, too.

Sucking in a gulp of air strong enough to strip the shelves of lipsticks, I squealed, "Oh, Mom, look! All the girls wear Ambush. It smells so good. Isn't the bottle pretty?"

My mother sniffed the tester bottle and winced. "If all the girls slap on a handful of this every day, I pity your poor teachers."

"Oh, Mo-om!" I laughed to humour her. "Can I have some, Mom? Please? Can I, can I, please?" I heard a sharp, desperate edge in my voice that hadn't been there, even when I was pleading for the jeans.

She checked the bottom of the bottle, then set it back with a clunk. "Thirty-eight fifty for this dinky little bottle? No way, Kendra. Forget it."

"You just want me to stink! No wonder I don't have any friends – "

"If you don't have any friends, it's not because you don't wear perfume. Did you ever think it might be your attitude?"

Once she started down this trail, I knew I'd never beat her. I had to head her off at the pass. "I'm the ugliest girl in school and it's all your fault! I look like those girls in prison films – all I need is one of those awful grey dresses!"

"Kendra, did you totally forget the rule? No begging? I've already spent a lot more than I intended. Where do you think money comes from?"

"From Daddy… some of it."

Her face grew dark. "Not that much, if you must know. And that's if his cheque is on time, which it is not this month. I'm leaving this shop, right now." She marched off down the aisle.

I stood firm, not budging a corpuscle. My mother stalked back a moment later, eyes blazing.

"Are you coming with me, young lady, or not?"

"Not." I folded my arms across my chest. "I'm not moving until you let me get a bottle of Ambush."

"What's got into you tonight? I ought to send

you to live with your father since you think life with me is so bad…"

I didn't jump right in and say, "Oh, no, Mom. I'm sorry I said that." I was too close to getting what I wanted so I just looked at her, round-eyed and innocent.

"Fine! I'm going, Kendra. I'm leaving you right here." She took a step towards the exit, calling my bluff.

Believe me, this was not fun. I missed the old days when my mother gave me two dollars a week. I'd blow it on plastic jewellery and some sweets and be as happy as a clam. Back then, I didn't care if I went out the door wearing fishing boots and my mother's old dressing gown, and I thought perfume smelled yucky.

Now my allowance is five dollars a week and I can't make ends meet. Being thirteen is no bed of roses.

Mom took a few more steps. She looked like she was actually going to leave me this time.

I trotted out Plan C.

"Daddy wouldn't say no," I said archly. "He'd let me get whatever I wanted."

"Is that so? Did your father pay for your school clothes? Has he put any money into your college fund?"

College was years away. I needed to be an MPG

now. That was all that mattered.

"Jennifer would buy me Ambush," I said. "She knows what's cool and what's important to kids like me." It was a mean, low-down card, but I had to play it.

What was left of my mother's patience crumbled. "You can have the small bottle, but don't spray that stuff on in the house. I don't have a gas mask."

She went up to the counter and wearily handed over her credit card. While the girl rang up the sale, Mom stood a little apart from me, looking as if she wished the nurse had switched babies in the hospital.

We headed out of the store, my mother walking a mile ahead of me. I didn't care. I had accomplished my mission.

As I mentally tallied my prizes, I felt a gritty sort of triumph. For the first time in my life, I realised I had a certain power over my mother. It was like that day a few months ago when we both noticed I was exactly her height, and could look her right in the eye.

"Here," she said, thrusting the bag at me. "I'd better not hear another peep out of you for the next month, is that clear?"

I nodded, nearly fainting with happiness as I clutched my precious purchases all the way out to the car.

I held the bag on my lap, not wanting to let my new things out of sight. Mom started the car without a word and drove out of the car park towards Route 28.

"Aren't we going to Banjo's?" I asked.

"I don't feel like going to Banjo's."

"How about Pancho Villa's, then?"

"I'm not hungry." She switched on the radio, discouraging any further conversation.

We headed back into the black night in a tense silence. I thought Mom would call Daddy about my revolting behaviour on our way home, but her mobile phone stayed in her bag. I knew that once we got home, she would close the door to her room and count the week's money on her bed, sorting the bills into little piles. She'd probably have to borrow from her emergency fund to make up what she had spent on me tonight.

We stared straight ahead through the windscreen into the darkness. I felt an invisible barrier had suddenly sprung up between us, like one of those smoked-glass window-dividers in limousines, and that we would be on opposite sides for a long time.

When we bumped over the Bull Run bridge, I forgot to cross my fingers. No big deal – I wasn't the same person as when we had gone over the bridge a few hours before. Was it a trick of the darkness, or was the road longer going home for once?

My favourite song came on. Josh Campbell's voice swirled inside our car, wreathing my head, wrapping me in sweet notes. In my fantasy, he was singing just to me.

I hugged my shopping bag, breathing softly to keep the magic from "Don't Look Back" from disappearing.

The Dolphin Bracelet

CAROLINE PITCHER

My dad held out his cupped hands, then opened them. Gold coins clattered down onto the table and lay glinting in the Greek sunshine.

Dad chuckled. He reached into his back pocket. He slapped down a wad of banknotes and smoothed them with his hands as if he was ironing them. Then he sat back, folded his arms and smirked.

Connor, my older brother, said, "That's your share, Mum."

"Yeah," said my other brother, Josh. "That's what's left. We've had flippers and masks and snorkels, state-of-the-art stuff – "

"And windsurfing lessons and diving lessons," said Connor. "So that's all yours, Mum."

It was like they'd done a bank job.

"What about me?" I cried.

"It's yours too, Jodie," said Dad. "Why don't you girls go shopping? We're going diving off that headland."

"Girls shop, boys dive? That's a bit of a gender

39

stereotype!" said Connor, who's talked funny ever since he's been at college.

"It's all right by me," said Mum.

Dad put his arm across her shoulders and pulled her gently to him.

"Get something really special, love," he said. He kissed her, a big wet smackeroo. Right on her mouth. They'd been doing that a lot lately. Connor said it was "excluding", and I agreed, although I didn't really know what he meant.

All that money. Just think what we could buy!

"Come on, Mum!" I cried. "Let's go down to the shops before it gets too hot."

"Let her finish her coffee, Jodie," said Dad.

So I stood at her shoulder, waiting for her to finish the tiny cupful. She said the coffee over here was like manure, but she sort of liked it.

Last time we went shopping together, we had to do a List. That was when I started secondary school. There were no surprises. Baggy shorts for games and PE, knee-length skirt, white blouses, even a tie, would you believe! Clumpy black shoes with heels as high as I could get Mum to pay for, a couple of sweatshirts, French dictionary, English dictionary, fountain pen, plastic wallets for my work, calculator, all that stuff! Mum wrote The List. She wrote it all in royal-blue ballpoint. I could have drawn a map of exactly where we had to go.

This morning, with so much cash, in a strange place, and no list, it was unreal. We didn't know where we were going, or what we were buying. Forward into the little Greek town, with all those euros. Retail fantasy! Heaven…

Arm in arm, we dawdled along the waterfront, past the boats rocking on the clear green water. We'd gone out on one of those boats a couple of days before. I'd thought I might be sick over the side, but it wasn't scary at all. I liked it. I liked the smell of the boat, petrol from the engine, salt from the sea and the dinner cooking in the galley underneath.

It was the best day of the holiday, I remembered as we turned down a little street. Maybe this one led to the shops? Overhead was a sort of trellis. Vines and pinky-purple flowers scrambled across and made a roof. They were called boogie-something-or-other, and they cast violet dapples on the cobblestones and kept you cool in their shade.

No pavements here. Hardly any cars either, because they'd have got stuck. The buildings were painted white – lovely, blinding white, not dingy white. When Mum was in the hospital, the walls looked yellow, as if the patients had been smoking sixty a day.

There were lots of doors in this little street. Most

of them were blue, all kinds of blues. Some of them were old doors, with the paint peeling off in tatters like nail varnish on a Monday morning, but you didn't really notice the tatty bits.

"The doors make me want to open them," I said. "If they were at home, they'd just look old and messy."

"It's the light," said Mum. "It's the way the sunlight comes off the sea. So clear." She stopped for a moment and closed her eyes. "Beautiful, isn't it?"

"Yeah. Wiz! Cashmere!" I told her.

It was special. I felt as if my feet made no sound as we walked along. As if there were feathers on my heels. This was my first foreign holiday. One night in May, Dad had come in, shouting, "Guess what I've just been and done?"

"What? WHAT?!" shouted Josh.

"Aha!" teased Dad, but Connor shook him by the shoulders till he burst out, "I've booked a holiday. For all of us!"

"Where, Dad, WHERE?!"

"Skiathos!"

Eh? We'd hoped for Florida, Disneyland, Lanzarote or Ibiza.

"So where is this Skiathos place?" frowned Connor.

"Greece. Lots of sun and sea. Restful for Mum

and me. Although I think there is a club for you lot…"

"For a week?" I asked.

"A fortnight."

Flabber? We were gasted! I suppose we could have asked why – but we didn't. I wanted to know why Josh and I were getting out of school, but I thought Dad might change his mind. So I kept quiet.

The holiday put a kind of spell on us. The sunlight and heat were dazzling. We slept late, lulled by the rhythm of the waves, swam and sunbathed all day, ate late in the evening at a taverna on the harbour side, where the soft lights shimmered on the black water. A lot of the time we sat and looked at the sea and the sky. There was so much of them. It was like being carried through a lovely dream, on one of those moving walkway things they have at airports.

Shops! I had forgotten until this morning that there were still things like shops. I'd been in the sea most of the holiday. What had Mum been doing? She was brown as a walnut. I say walnut, because you could see her crinkles. She was also thinner than usual. I wasn't. Too many free ice creams from Yiorgos, the fit waiter at the pool bar. The boat captain was called Yiorgos, too. (Yiorgos means George. There were lots of Georges.)

"Here's a shop, Mum!" I cried.

It sold everything – olives in buckets, lotions for tourists' sunburn and prickly heat, little gold-and-blue tins of thyme honey. I pawed my way along the rack of T-shirts with the names of the Greek football team set out on the back. Blue and white, the colours of victory. We bought my brothers one each.

"No, not for your dad," said Mum. She pulled out one with a logo of the Olympic rings instead.

I ransacked the shelves piled with fringed sarongs and tried on the silver rings. I didn't really know what I was looking for. Nothing was quite right. I caught sight of my mother's little frown and knew I was right.

"Bit naff?" I whispered.

"Tourist tat," she said. "We're after something better."

Out in the sunlight we blinked at the white walls. My mum put on her sunglasses again and said, "Let's stop for a drink."

"Already?" I asked.

We sat under a blue-and-white awning. Across the narrow street were pots. In each pot was a little lemon tree, with white blossoms and a lemon or two. The blossom was the sweetest thing I have ever smelled.

A man with a moustache like a broom appeared at Mum's side.

"Kalimera," she said. "Two freshly squeezed orange juices please — and hey, how about a sticky pastry, Jodie? Baklava?"

Baklava? I thought that was a knitted hood thing toddlers and terrorists wore. But I was up for anything sticky!

The island was slowly waking up. There were more people around. A family came stomping in under the awning, sighing in the heat. They plonked themselves down at the next table. There was a red-faced woman in big orange shorts. She kept puffing, as if she was too hot. She had a scowling daughter and a lanky son. Their sad dad was last. He had such a long baggy T-shirt on, it looked as if he'd forgotten his shorts.

"Look! No knickers!" I sniggered.

"How could she let him go out looking like that!" whispered Mum.

Sometimes my mum and I got fits of giggles. No real reason. We just were on the same giggle-length. The big woman and the daughter stared at us. The big woman began drumming her fingers, waiting to be served.

A voice from the dark depths of the kitchen called "Yiorgos!" Another George. He brought us our baklavas and fresh orange. I attacked my pile of pastry and nuts, dripping with honey, like there was no tomorrow. Well, there might not be time for any tomorrow because we had to leave for the airport. I had to finish Mum's baklava for her, as she couldn't manage more than a couple of forkfuls. Then my straws got blocked with the bits of orange and I had to make a lot of noise sucking them through. More staring.

The woman snapped her fingers at Yiorgos. He acted like he didn't notice. I'd never seen anyone look through someone with such style! The scowly daughter said something cross. The mother was cross back. It was foreign talking. Not English.

Daughter's turn. She leaned across the table, sneered at her red mother, then flung herself back in her chair and stuck her bottom lip out so far you could have kept your CD collection on it. I tried not to stare, or to meet my own mother's eyes.

A thin ginger cat snaked towards our table.

"I wonder where she's got her kittens?" said Mum. "She's still feeding them. Just look at her underneath!"

I did. It was a bit of a shock. The cat opened her pink mouth and mewed soundlessly up at me. She wound herself around my ankles. It tickled.

"Sorry, I've nothing left," I said.

My mother smiled at Yiorgos. He came over. She pointed to something on the menu. He nodded, but looked a little puzzled. There was Silent Staring from the next table. Then the daughter said something to her mother that sounded mouthy. She got slapped! Ow! That's right, slapped, on her arm.

A plate of glistening little fish arrived in front of Mum. She thanked Yiorgos graciously. The minute his back was turned, she trotted across the road and tipped all the tiny fish behind the lemon tree. The cat scampered after her and gnawed hungrily, every so often glancing over her shoulder, ears back.

The woman tutted. She stood up and barked a command to her family. Chairs scraped. They left. Her bottom rolled wildly in the orange shorts.

"Like two Halloween pumpkins," I said. "Pumpkin bum!"

"Don't be naughty, Jodie," spluttered Mum, trying to do a cross-parent bit, but we giggled, making each other worse until we were helpless, and she had to go inside the taverna and ask where the toilet was.

While I waited for her, I remembered. All that money! Maybe we should split it fifty-fifty, like a pair of robbers? That would be fair.

"Hey, Mum, let's just split the money!" I cried when she reappeared.

"Why don't we just see if we find anything we really want?" she said.

That sounded all right, too. I might find

something very expensive. Mum might be happy with something cheap. If I was lucky.

Down a little alleyway, we found The Right Shop. Well, Mum found it. I might not have gone through the doorway. Inside was so dark after the sunlight, you couldn't tell what you were letting yourself in for. There were glass cases full of jewellery, painted seascapes and views of the island on the wall, a wooden hand with tapering fingers trailing silky scarves, fine lacy mats and shelves that gleamed with coloured glass. There were signs saying things like "Handmade" and "Local Artist".

"That means expensive," said Mum.

I wandered past arty-looking pots decorated with charging bulls and bare men in olive wreaths, and gold-and-red icon paintings of dark faces and haloes. There was one of St George on his prancing white horse, with a very un-Greek castle behind him, pinning down a green dragon with his lance.

"Look, Mum!" I cried. "It's yet another Yiorgos!"

Very quickly, I saw what I wanted. It was a pendant, a drop of pale-blue stone on a thin chain. And there were earrings to match, loops with the same pale-blue stone, blue as the sky. Just my colour! Sometimes you see something and it calls out to you, doesn't it? It's just for you. Just right.

"Hey, Mum! I've found it!" I cried.

She came over. "That's lovely," she said.

She wandered away again, searching, while I did a recce of the other jewellery. Just to check. There was some cool stuff, but nothing so good. I'd made the right choice, first time.

Or so I thought…

Mum was hunched over a glass case. I scooted across to her and announced, "I have made my decision."

"I've decided too," she breathed. "I've found the perfect thing. It will be as if I'm taking this holiday home with me. Look! next to that tray of rings … "

I saw at once what she was after. It was a bracelet. It was slender, with a design all the way around the silver. Small shapes were cut into it and filled with pale bluey-green, and deep blue, and white. Each shape linked with the one before and the one after.

Dolphins. They swam nose to tail, on and on, around the bracelet. That was what Mum wanted, but I wanted it too. My mind cried, *I am the child. I am the daughter. I'm supposed to have things, aren't I?* That bracelet was the very best thing to take home from this holiday. Why? We had watched them from Yiorgos's boat that special day. He followed them out to sea for us. He switched off the engine and signalled to us to sit still and be quiet. We sat there, breathless, rocking on the waves, watching them. Dolphins in their tight skins, playing, bounding, leaping, gleaming in the sunlight. They curled through the air like silver rings from a Christmas-cracker puzzle.

It was the first time any of us had seen dolphins.

Later that day, we'd gone snorkelling and swimming, me in my plastic shoes in case of those spiky sea-urchin things. Mum was just sitting on the beach. Once, I had come splashing and shouting out of the sea, back to her.

She was crying.

"What's the matter, Mum? Have you been stung?" I asked, because lots of stinging things bigger than I'd ever seen whizzed around this island. We had to put mozzie zappers in the electric sockets at night, and there were jellyfish floating in the sea like big hairnets.

She shook her head. Wiped her eyes and nose. "Nothing's the matter, Jodie," she said. "It's perfect. Everything." I had sat next to her for a while and held her hand.

Now, in this shop, she said "You want the bracelet, don't you? Well, maybe there are two..." but the shop woman shook her head. She unlocked the glass cabinet and took out the bracelet, handing it carefully to my mum.

"What is that deep blue stone?" asked Mum.

"Lapis lazuli," said the shop woman.

"Lapis lazuli…" repeated Mum in a whisper. "Doesn't that sound beautiful?"

Yes. It did. I ran my fingers round the silver and touched the little dolphins. They were made of turquoise and mother-of-pearl, and this deep blue lapis-lazuli stuff. The dolphins were nose to tail. Swimming round the bracelet. On and on, round and round, endlessly.

Mum gave a funny little smile. Her face looked sort of weary and beaten. She said "We've enough money… We can get the necklace you like, and this bracelet too. I can get something else… I'd like to think of you wearing the dolphins."

I didn't say anything but my mind was busy, working like a slide show. It started with a picture of the pumpkin-bottom family. The sneers, the silences and the stinging slap. Next, a picture of me. I didn't like it very much. I looked young. I was scowling. The corners of my mouth turned down, all sullen and petulant and my bottom lip stuck out.

The next slide replaced that sullen one and it was much better. It was a girl – almost a woman - with a calm half-smile. Wise or what?!

This wise girl said, in a low, slow voice, "Guess what? I was right the first time. I'd like the necklace and earrings, please. They are my colour. You have the dolphin bracelet."

I got a real kick from saying that.

"Jodie, love — " she began, but I wasn't having any.

"No," I said. "No arguing, Mum."

At last she said, "All right, then. But you can wear the bracelet when I don't."

"That's more than fair," I said.

She paid, counting out the golden euros and the crisp banknotes.

"There's some left," she said. "So let's get that little icon picture to remind us of all those Georges."

The shop woman fussed and packed the jewellery in pretty boxes with ribbons and gift-wrapped St George in sheaves of classy tissue paper.

The minute we were out Mum and I went on for ice cream (sweet vanilla, raspberry and chocolate, and yes, you've guessed it, I had most of Mum's). A different café this time, with purple trumpets of morning glory flowers swarming and tootling all over the roof.

We undid the ribbons on the boxes and decked ourselves out. Mum fastened my necklace for me and I put on the earrings. They made me hold my head up high, gracefully (I hoped). I fastened the dolphins around her wrist. We sat there, smiling every now and then. The shadows melted as the sun rose even higher. An emerald-green lizard scurried away into the wall.

I realised Time doesn't tick on just the same. It had just leaped forward, even on this hot late morning when things seemed to stop. *I have jumped into somewhere very clear...*

And after a while we wandered back and tracked down Dad and my brothers. Three little periscopes, out by the rocks. Dad surfaced. We waved and in they swam.

We went for late lunch, for Greek salad, tzatziki and chips, served, of course, by gorgeous Yiorgos. I thought of the little gold-and-red George and his dragon. They were going on our mantelpiece when we got home, to remind us of all the Georges we had met here.

Mum went for a sleep. I got my bikini, stashed away the necklace and earrings and nipped back to the beach for a sizzle in the sea.

That evening the five of us went out for a supper under the stars. We listened to the sea stroking the pebbly beach. Somewhere out there the dolphins were swimming in the vast dark sea.

❊ ❊ ❊

It was the day after we got back that Dad told us why they had spent so much money on a holiday.

Mum was ill again. It was three whole years since she was first ill. Now the doctors said, *We are very sorry, but the remission is over.*

So my dad had gone for it, taken out all his savings and spent the lot. Dreamtime together. In case the chance didn't come again.

And it didn't.

I suppose I had pushed Mum's illness away in my mind, because I didn't want to keep thinking about it. Although I hadn't pushed it right to the back, had I?

Mum wore that bracelet every minute of every night and day, until it was time to take it off and give it to me.

Now I wear it. The dolphins swim round and round my wrist, too, and I love them.

Making It Up

JULIA JARMAN

She is SO annoying.

"Polly, do you really want to go?"

"Yes, Mum, I want to go ice-skating." I say it firmly. I have no doubts.

"Who else is going?"

"Melanie."

That look crosses her face. She doesn't like Melanie. She thinks Melanie is "forward".

"But darling, what if…"

"Mum, I want to go!"

But do I? There are butterflies in my stomach now. Butterflies? Frogs, more like, leaping about and doing somersaults – and she put them there. Or maybe, to be fair, she just fed the tiny tadpole doubts that were already there. That's what she does – so that suddenly a good idea seems like a not-so-good idea. *What if?* How I hate those words.

Mum, I'd like my ears pierced.

But, darling, what if they get infected?

Now I see myself, clinging to the rail around the

rink, making a fool of myself. What if I can't skate? What if I fall over and break a leg? What if Melanie has arranged to meet someone else there — a boy — and the two of them don't want me around? What if they go off and leave me? I see myself stranded in the middle of the rink. See everyone jeering. What would I wear? How would I get there? And get back? I'd have to ask for a lift, and Mum or Dad would turn up half an hour before pick-up time in the Skoda. It's easier to stay at home.

We stay at home a lot, my family and me. Other families go on adventure holidays — pony-trekking, or white-water rafting. They fly to foreign locations. Mum's scared of flying. Melanie's family flies all over the world, seeking out the tallest, fastest rollercoasters with the most sudden drops. They collect rollercoasters. Other families go to Alton Towers, at the very least. We must be the only family who has never, ever been, though I went last week, on a school trip, despite the "What ifs".

I asserted myself that time. "YES, Mum! I really want to go!"

I pleaded. "Mum, Dad, EVERYONE in my class is going!"

Dad signed the permission form. He's not quite as bad as Mum, though he does side with her against me, more than he does against Malc. Malc is, of course, a boy, and must therefore be a boy, and boys take risks. They play rough games and have adventures.

If I hadn't gone to Alton Towers, I'd never have heard the last of it from the other girls. Girls. Oh yes. Of course I go to a girls-only school. As soon as I was eleven, Mum and Dad said they didn't want me mixing with boys, or rough girls. They don't think there are rough girls at St Hilda's, which shows how out of touch they are.

Alton Towers was great. The frogs quietened down a bit after a couple of rides. I went on everything – Oblivion, Nemesis, everything. On the Cork Screw, I screamed with terror, and so did Melanie, who was clinging to me with her eyes tight shut, I noted. I was SO proud of myself afterwards – but when I got home, Mum didn't want to know.

"Don't tell me, Polly." She closed her eyes and covered her ears. "It makes me ill, just thinking about it."

I think Mum's even more afraid of heights than she's scared of boys looking at me. And I'm not that bothered – about boys I mean. The few I've met – mostly Malc's friends – haven't impressed. They're younger than me, for a start. I wouldn't dream of dating any of them. And I feel a bit sorry for Mum about the heights thing; it's a phobia and she can't do anything about it.

Correction. *Felt* a bit sorry for her. Things changed yesterday – because she's been reading my diary! Can you believe it? She's been spying on me! Why am I so sure? Well, I wasn't at first, though I had this feeling when I came back from school and found the bottom drawer of my dressing table closed. That's where I keep my diary, and I'd left it open because Purr – that's my gorgeous, golden, fluffy cat – loves sleeping there at the moment, AND because I didn't think anyone would snoop. Didn't think my own mother would stoop so low. In short, I trusted her – and thought she trusted me. Also, frankly, there's nothing much to hide. But what if there *was* something I wanted to keep private? It's the principle.

So today I checked. I left a speck of grit by the T in Tuesday on the left-hand page. When I came home from school, the grit had rolled into the crease between the two pages. Proof! No, it wasn't Purr. She sleeps at the front of the drawer. My diary was right at the back. When I asked Purr if Mum had been foraging, she looked up at me, and her gorgeous green eyes glinted knowingly. My first impulse was to rush downstairs and throttle Mum, but then I had a better idea – give her something to worry about!

If she reads my diary again, she'll find it a bit more interesting – very interesting, in fact.

Oh, I'm not going to do anything stupid. I'm not daft. I'm not going to prove her point by putting myself at risk. But I am going to make up something that could give her the heebie-jeebies. I'm not even going to write about anything remotely dangerous. She wouldn't be able to stop herself if I did. She'd flip, tell Dad, alert the emergency services and/or lock me up in a tower. No, I'm just going to give her enough to niggle her. Hint that I've got a boyfriend perhaps? Or a secret admirer! That would be enough to make her sweat, but not enough to make her wade in. I'm going to have to think about this carefully.

This should do for starters:

Wednesday 15th September
School OK. Got an A for English. Melanie asked me again about ice-skating on Friday. She can go if I can. Her mum says she'll take if mine collects.

I think X fancies me. He tried to catch my eye, but I ignored him. He's dreamy-looking – long eyelashes – and very funny – ha ha not weird – but he's a bit old for me and I don't think I want a boyfriend yet.

Note, I didn't say who. I didn't say where. And I

reassured her that I wasn't interested. There's just enough there to get her going – it gives me time to think up a few details, too – and prove how sensible I am. I don't want to stymie my chance of going ice-skating. Later, I asked her about it and she said she'd see if Dad could collect me because she's not keen on driving into town at night.

Thursday 16th September
Yippee! Mum says I can go skating. Dad will collect. I love her to bits.

That should encourage her. Note how positive I am, and how I didn't even mention my secret admirer. In fact, if she responds to encouragement and becomes more reasonable, I might have to abandon my plan. Pity, in a way – I was growing quite fond of lover boy.

Friday 17th September
Ice-skating was great. Jeans and glittery vest-top were OK. Melanie was really nice. She didn't meet anyone else there and she taught me how to do it. She IS a bossy-boots, but by the end of the session I could get from one side of the rink to the other without falling over, and she said she'll teach me how to turn around next week. Dad

bought us fish and chips on the way home.

But then he spoiled it by getting all concerned when Melanie's mum wasn't in when she got home. She let herself in with her own key. Of course, he told Mum, who went into overdrive on the anxiety front. I said, "Most 12-year-olds have their own key, you know." And Mum said, "But what if...?" OTT isn't the phrase; she goes over the top and up the other side again. But I haven't given up trying for Friday night.

<u>Saturday 18th September</u>
Boring. Mum noticed a bruise on my arm and wondered if we should go to Casualty. "What if it's a break, darling?" It's nice that she cares, but I do wish Mum wouldn't worry so much. My arm is fine.

<u>Sunday 19th September</u>
Did Maths homework in morning. Hope I got it right. But two minuses make a plus? I don't get that. Rest of day boring — and VERY upsetting. Heard Mum telling Gran — we went to Gran's for lunch — about me going ice-skating, and Gran started what-if-ing even worse than Mum. Now I see where she gets it from. Mum told Gran she didn't think she'd let me go next Friday. I just hope she changes her mind. She will if she

cares about our relationship. Melanie IS a responsible person, and so are her parents — her mum works in a care home for old people — but they TRUST her. I think trust is VERY important between mother and daughter. Perhaps if Mum got out more, and didn't just sit at home with her patchwork, worrying?

Plenty of hints there, but she didn't take them. Actually, I could have filled pages with FURY and INDIGNATION. On the way home from Gran's, I asked her outright, and she said she hadn't made up her mind yet, but I'm sure she has. She said it isn't right that Melanie goes home to an empty house. Now she's worrying about Melanie, too. I said that if we didn't go, Melanie would be on her own all evening, but she didn't follow the logic of that. She said, why didn't I get a friend from a nice family? She really is asking for it.

<u>Monday 20th September</u>
I am desolated. When I got home from school today, Mum said, "Let's discuss Friday night, darling." Then proceeded to TELL me that I can't go ice-skating on Friday.

Right! My love affair is going to hot up!

Tuesday 21st September
Saw X today TWICE! Caught him looking at me with his big brown eyes. He has ever such long lashes. He's really hunky. And he's only three years older than me. He's doing his GCSEs — eleven of them. So he has brains and brawn. Plays for the First Eleven. Melanie says he really, really fancies me, but I should play hard to get. I AM hard to get.

Wednesday 22nd September
X asked me to go out with him. When I said I was too busy — I DIDN'T say I wasn't allowed, cos I would've looked daft — he asked if he could ring me. I said only if he didn't mind MI5 listening in.

Ha! The interrogation has started — on Wednesday, as soon as I got home from school — and she thinks she's being oh so subtle!

"Darling..." so casually as she peeled potatoes, "did you talk to anyone on the bus today?"

"Just the usual crowd."

She's deduced that my secret lover must be someone on the school bus, because St Hilda's and St Edward's use the same one. She was dead worried about that when she first heard about it and wanted to take me by car, but has been a bit more relaxed about it since Malc started at St Edward's. He's there too, so I can't be abducted. My ten-year-old protector! He's smaller than me! I bet she interrogates Malc – and, of course, he won't tell her a thing!

She has. I heard her, while he was trying to watch TV. And I heard him saying that he sat at the front of the bus with his mates, he wasn't interested in what I was doing, and he supposed I talked non-stop to Melanie and Deeta as usual on the back seat. The bus picks up from St Hilda's first and we always grab the back seat. He said we never stop talking and NO, I hadn't got a boyfriend. Now she thinks we're both deceiving her!

The plot thickens. Malc's best mate, Blake, who happens to be Deeta's brother, came round tonight – to see Malc's new Gameboy. I was in the sitting room, half-watching EastEnders, with a mag on my knee, and he – Blake, that is – said, "Believe that stuff, do you?"

It was open at a feature on palm-reading. "Course I do. I'm an expert."

He laughed and held out his hand, "Read my future then."

"Cross my palm with silver."

He gave me 50p and I took his hand. "Right. Oh dear. Are you ready for this? Your lifeline looks very very short."

He laughed again as Mum came in.

Her eyes bulged and she went scarlet.

"P-Polly, come and help with the washing-up." Her voice was tight, almost a squeak.

"Mum, we've got a dishwasher."

"Polly!"

She thinks she's on to something. As I left the room, I noticed that Blake has very long eyelashes.

When we reached the kitchen, she cast around for something for me to do. There were a couple of pans on the draining board.

"Dry those, please."

I ignored the tea cloth in her hand. "What's up, Mum?"

"Flaunting yourself!" she hissed.

"Mum, I was pretending to read his palm."

"With a spotty youth!"

"Mum, he's eleven and his name's Blake and I thought you liked him." I've heard her saying the Parkers were a nice family. She likes Deeta.

"So that's…" She stopped herself.

"That's what?"

She didn't answer. Didn't need to. It was obvious. She thought Blake was lover boy! She is definitely still reading my diary, but not very carefully. Well, if that's what she wants to think…

"I'm going upstairs to do my homework."

I went straight to my diary, but thought hard before I wrote. She'd read this tomorrow while I was at school. Worry her too much, and she'd meet me out of school. But if she did, I could give her the slip! There is a side exit. Then what would she do? Follow the school bus, probably, thinking I must be on it. And when I didn't get off at the other end? She'd panic! Ring Dad certainly. Ring the school. Ring the police, maybe? Possibly. And then I'd turn up, after catching the public bus home! "Sorry, everyone, I missed the school bus."

She'd look SO silly.

Or… Yes, I've an even better idea!

Thursday 23rd September

Mum was SO embarrassing last night. She thought little Blake Parker was my boyfriend. She came in as I was pretending to read his palm, and acted as if she'd found us snogging. As if I would – with him! With X though? Maybe. He's yummy and has asked me to meet him after school tomorrow – at St Cuthbert's Church. He goes to the youth club there and says there's a marvellous view from the top of the tower. Not sure yet if I'll go, but I'm tempted.

Top of the tower! Stroke of genius, that, but pause for

a think. When she reads that, she'll definitely try to meet me out of school, so I'll have to leave by the side exit. Then what? Will she follow the school bus home, or go straight to St Cuthbert's? I haven't said I'm going there, so I think she'll go home first to see if I'm there. And if I'm not? She'll race round to the church, thinking I'm up the tower with my secret lover. I can just see her standing at the bottom, a wobbling jelly, too scared to go up. Well, actually, she won't be able to go up – churches are all locked these days – and I'm not that cruel; I'd put her out of her misery after watching her quake for a few minutes. She'd probably search the churchyard, thinking I was snogging lover boy on top of a tombstone, and I'd spring out from behind one and say, "Let that be a lesson to you. DON'T read my diary and DON'T treat me like a child and DON'T act as if you can't trust me!"

❦ ❦ ❦

The plan was working! During the last lesson of the day I saw her from the second-floor window of the Art Room, waiting for me outside the main entrance. Hope no one recognised her – I'd die of embarrassment. She must have parked around the corner. The road was full of school buses. As soon as the bell went, I headed for the side entrance and the bus stop.

First snag – the bus took ages to come. I kept expecting Mum to drive by in the car, looking for me, but she didn't.

Second snag – the bus, when it did come, took ages. It must have stopped at every stop. Can't believe it took so long. Think the driver was on a go-slow. I could see the square tower of the church long before it got there, and scaffolding round it. At the rate the bus was going, Mum would get there before me. She'd probably be waiting at the gate, and my plan would be thwarted.

She wasn't there but her car was – on the road in front of the gate, on a yellow line. Not worried about a parking ticket, then. I paused for a moment. Was she in it? No. I tried the car door and it opened. Not worried about thieves. She must have rushed inside in a real panic – about ME.

Cautiously, I stepped into the churchyard. Was she there?

Not that I could see. I still fancied jumping out from behind a tombstone, and had spotted a tall one made of black marble, when I noticed the church door was open. Not locked, then. Odd, that. Had Mum gone inside? Still keeping a lookout, I hurried up the path and peeped inside – and the scent of flowers hit me. The church was full of flowers, as if someone had decorated it for a wedding. A mountainous arrangement in pink and white stood on the font by the door. I stepped inside. Definitely a wedding. White bows decorated the pew ends, and there was a half-finished arrangement near the pulpit. Where was the arranger? I expected to see someone foraging on the ground for more flowers, or getting water from the chancel where there was a modern sink-unit, but there was no one around.

"Mum . . . " I don't know why I whispered her name, but the impulse to take her by surprise had ebbed a bit – even before I saw the sign that read TO BELL TOWER.

She wouldn't have.

She couldn't have!

There was a notice below it saying TOWER CLOSED FOR RENOVATION. But when I reached the vestry, at the bottom of the tower, I could see an open door. Beyond it, narrow stone steps spiralled upwards. Red-and-white plastic tape dangled from a hook on the wall. A barrier with a sign saying DANGER had been pushed to one side, and there was something looped over it – Mum's duffel coat. I had a picture of her in my mind, taking it off – she must have thought she was too fat to climb the spiral stairs – and then gathering her strength to make the ascent.

I started to climb.

Up and up and round and round I went, expecting at every turn to find her sitting, trembling, on the steps. A cold wind streamed down from above. The stairway was very narrow. She might even be stuck.

Up and up I went.

I passed the bells, lying on their sides, their open mouths like caves.

I came to an open door, could see clouds scudding by, framed by scaffolding. I stepped outside, onto a narrow ledge, and the wind whipped my hair over my face. Only a handrail stood between me and the ground below. I took a fleeting look.

It seemed to rush up to meet me.

I felt sick.

She wouldn't have.

She couldn't have.

I pressed my back against the wall. Didn't want to go any further.

"Mum!"

I felt the wind catch my words, hurling them into the air and over the treetops. No answer.

From the corner of my right eye, I saw the grey stone wall of the tower, and estimated that it was about five metres to the corner. Then, clutching the rail with both hands, I side-shuffled towards it, school skirt clinging to my legs. The wind howled. I turned the corner, made myself actually walk the next five-metre stretch. And the next. Then I saw her – well, I saw hands above me, clutching the battlements, or what looked like battlements – and hair blowing in the wind.

But I couldn't see how she'd got up there.

"Mum!"

The wind carried my voice away. I don't think she heard me.

"Mum, how did – " I shouted. Suddenly I noticed the rusty ladder leading up to the top of the wall.

Dare I?

She'd dared.

I dared.

Up and up.

And then – she must have heard or seen me – there was Mum's white face directly above, hands outstretched.

She almost pulled me over the wall at the top and I fell into her arms. I didn't know what to say. I could feel her trembling – or was that me?

I pulled away. I was still furious. "How could you be so stupid?"

But she wasn't listening to me. She was looking at the top of the ladder – for my boyfriend.

I shouted, "He's not coming! I haven't got one!"

She looked puzzled.

I said, "Boyfriend. I made him up, because you read my diary."

She looked at her feet. Guilty as charged.

I did enjoy that moment for a bit, but another feeling was nudging it to one side. I didn't want her to look small and ashamed.

"It's all right, Mum." I touched her arm. "I know why."

She loved me. She'd climbed up here, though she was terrified – for me. She cared about me more than she cared for herself.

I felt as small as the creepy-crawly creepy-crawling up the wall beside her.

"I sh-shouldn't have, Polly." She was still trembling.

I put my arm round her. "And I shouldn't have lied."

"N-no, I was wrong. I should have known better."

"We were both wrong – but it's turned out all right."

As this love-in continued, I had a thought. *Two minuses make a plus. I've got it at last.*

"Yes," she said, "if it hadn't been for you, I'd never have seen this wonderful view. It's like a patchwork quilt."

I had another thought – that this was too good to last.

"The sky's like a sheet of gold," said Mum, "and look at those red berries glistening against the green..."

It was a now-or-never moment. I said, "About Friday..."

"Oh Polly..."

I took her hand. "If you're still worried about Melanie, couldn't she come back for a sleep-over?"

"Polly, let's discuss this when we get down."

"Discuss, like two people expressing opinions?"

"Yes, Polly."

Going down was worse than going up, in some ways – my knees were knackered when we got to the bottom – but no pain without gain. On the way home, we really talked – and I'll soon be doing double axels at the rink!

Snow-Globe Moment

SHIRLEY KLOCK

My gram collects snow globes – crystal balls with little scenes frozen inside. Flakes of snow drift over the scene when you shake it. Even though they are called snow globes, not all have snow. Some are filled with glitter, golden or silver, or even confetti, like tiny petals. When I think back over the good things I want to remember, I count out what I call my snow-globe moments, scenes from my own life that I want to keep forever. Some people might write them down in a journal or something, but I'm not much for writing. This month I've been getting out my memory snow globes a lot. They help me to feel better.

Here's one from not too long ago:

Mother and I stand on top of Windy Hill. But there's no wind, not a breath. The hot yellow fields fall away, dotted with oak groves. Her arm is around me. I stare into that scene. Then I shake my head, and flakes of sky and sunshine float around our shoulders. We had pounded up that dusty trail. I felt good – in the Zone or getting there. Yeah. Muscles elastic, just eating up the dust with my trail shoes. We moved faster when we were certain we were heading in the right direction, and the air cooled my sweaty skin as we rushed through it.

A hot spot tried to drill a hole in the balloon of my well-being. I needed to stop, but it felt too good to keep going. I'd been breaking in a new pair of trail shoes, and now I felt a blister coming on my heel. I had duct tape in my pocket. When we got to the next control point, I'd get the shoe off and tape the spot. Without slowing, I checked the folded square I held in my right hand. According to the map, the control should be just up ahead.

But it wasn't. We accelerated through a grove of oaks – ahhh, shade! – and out into the open. "Great view," panted Mom, bending over, hands on knees. "Water," she croaked. She was out of shape, but definitely improving.

"Yeah," I said. We could see the valley below us: the line of smog below the far hills, the marshy edges of the Bay. But... I steadied my thumb compass against the map. "The control should be..." I turned, letting the compass needle quiver to a stop. "Uh-oh."

Water gurgled as Mother gulped. "Ahh," she said, recapping the bottle, "What? What's wrong?"

"Umm, back there, at that last trail junction," I

gestured down the hill, where the dusty trail baked under the cloudless sky.

Mom knew immediately what had happened. I'd got us messed up before. She groaned. "Rashida! Back before we started up this mountain? A 180-degree error! Again!" That's what it's called when you manage to get yourself turned around completely. We both stared down the hill.

"I can see it," whispered Mom. She was right – down the hill, in the opposite direction, the orange-and-white bag was just visible.

"Shoot," I said. "It's downhill. Should be easy."

"For you," groaned Mom. "I don't know which my knees dread more, up or down. And, this extra – what? – mile? I blame you. Absolutely."

I shrugged. "I told you to navigate. But no…"

"This is a mind-and-body sport, girl," she said, and groaned. "My poor thigh muscles."

"Yeah, I know. Poor Mom! Hey, I've got an idea! You be the mind. I'll take care of the body part." Back when we first started this sport, she'd coaxed me, saying, "Come on, Rashida, you'll love orienteering. Lots of physical stuff. But you'll be using your mind, and I'll have to use my muscles. It'll be good for both of us."

I knew she wanted me to stretch my brain, just like she was stretching her muscles. She did that now, bouncing a little.

She straightened. "I'm gonna kill you," she decided suddenly. I stared at her, pulling down the brim of my cap, and backing away. "You still have water in your pack?" she asked.

I nodded. "Why?"

"Good," she said. And, before I could move, she poured what remained of hers right over my head. The droplets streaked across my skin, and I laughed out loud.

"Feels good," I said, and whipped my dreads around so that the water flicked across her too, like I was our dog shaking after a bath. Her arm fell across my shoulder, and we both grinned.

Yeah. That was nice. A real snow-globe moment from back in the good old days of summer. Now it's November, all of a sudden, and I'm living with Dad. Just Dad. We "got" the house, so I wouldn't have to change schools. Mom has her own place. Me? I can't seem to get my bearings. It's not just a one-eighty error. It's like my compass needle won't stop quivering all around the dial. I used to know right where I fit: in the centre, my mom on one side and Dad on the other. Balanced. Now everything is lop-sided!

Like this morning, I come downstairs, feeling pretty good. And what happens? I reach into the fridge for a yoghurt, and there's the family calendar on the door. Thursday, that's today, and in red it says "Mrs Porter". Mrs Porter is my sixth-grade teacher. My parents are supposed to meet with her. And me, too. After school. Not going to be a snow-globe moment; I know that already. Things have got out of hand. Talk about losing your sense of direction on the orienteering course. This whole first term of school has been like I started out with the map upside down, and just never recovered.

I'm standing there, staring at the note, when there's this crash from the garage. I go out there.

And she's there. Yes! Mom. Up on a ladder, filling a box with books from the overflow shelves Dad put up out there. My stupid heart actually leaps into my throat, and I have to calm down before I can speak. "What are you doing here?" Staring up at her, I can't help a little song that's starting my toes tapping: She's back! She's back!

"Well, good morning to you, too, gal," she says, looking down at me.

I cross my arms, and she sighs.

"My new place, it has wall-to-wall bookcases," she says, her voice warm. "Finally, I have a place for all my . . . " she trailed off. My mom is a professor of communications at Foothill College. Books are her thing. Not mine.

"So, you're not moving back in or anything," I say flatly.

She looks startled. "Oh, no, honeychild, I…" But I have already turned away. Now I know why Dad left so early. It wasn't that there was an early practice for the high school soccer team he coaches. It was so he wouldn't be here while she was in the house. She climbs down and follows me into the kitchen.

"Sorry, girl," she says softly. I don't answer, and she changes the subject. "Is that all you're having for breakfast?" I shrug. She frowns and looks me up and down.

"Don't worry," I say, "I'm not turning into scarecrow girl." I flex a muscle. "See?"

"MMM-hmm. Super Woman!" I want to laugh with her, but I can't. I'll only miss her more. So I don't.

Then it hits me. Parent-teacher conference. Conference day at school? Doesn't that mean… no classes? I think it does! I grab the school calendar from the bulletin board. Oh yeah! Yes! I do my little joy dance. School has never been my favourite thing. Well, breaktime and PE are okay, but the rest I can do without. Then I notice Mom smiling at me. And that stops me cold. I clear my throat and open the cutlery drawer. "What?" she asks.

"Nothing." Then I take pity on her and explain,

"No school. It's conference day," I say.

"Oh, right," she nods. "I was going to talk to you about that." She pauses. "I made a separate appointment to meet with your teacher, on my own."

I put the yoghurt and spoon on the table in a quiet, controlled way. Both of my parents always come to my conference. We always sit together, with me in the middle. I'd be the one with the butterflies kicking up a storm in my stomach. Mom would be calm and kind. Dad – well, Dad would just have this look of disbelief on his face. His moustache would start to bristle. He wasn't that great a student himself, Gram says. Maybe that's why he wants me to be better. I don't know. But, let's face it; I am not the world's best student. For some reason, Mom, who loves the school stuff, is more realistic about it. She just says, "All we ask is that you do your best." And, usually, I did that. I was solid. I did the work. I turned it in. Hearing that would settle Dad down.

But not this time. "You won't be there?" I said.

"I thought I'd let your father go with you today. We'll trade off."

I knew why, too. It was because they didn't want to be together. Not even for me. But I really, really wanted them both there. Especially this time. When they saw my sorry report card, it would be like doing a position check on the orienteering course. They'd both turn in the same direction. My direction! "I want you to come with Dad and me. Today."

"Look, 'Shida-child, I know this isn't what you want. But it isn't all about you. It really isn't."

But shouldn't it be about me? All about me? I'm not good enough, not important enough to keep their attention! I want to be their magnetic North. Their needles should point to me! Together! Right at me! Until I'm all grown up. That's how it should be. I think this so loudly in my head that I can hear myself saying it.

I look at Mom. "So when I get married, do I have to do it twice – once for you, once for Dad?"

She looks stricken.

"Never mind," I say and exit, but with dignity. Swish! Two points for me!

I throw myself on the bed, and stare at the autographed photo of the Stanford Women's Basketball team: strong women, all of them. Some day, my best friend Raynee and I, we were going to play college basketball together. She was going to have a growth spurt; I was going to get an athletic scholarship that would make up for my average grades. We were counting on it. No athletic scholarship though, will make up for the marks I'm getting this time around. I pick up my phone and punch in her number.

I haven't told anyone about anything yet. Seems like maybe I should start with Raynee.

She answers immediately. "Wassup?"

"You'll never, never guess. Not in a million years," I say, thinking of a way to tell her.

"Hmm." She pauses, thinking. "Your parents are getting a divorce?" she asks.

I almost hang up. Instead, I splutter, "How did you know?"

"Wha-a-t? I'm right?" she squeals and laughs. Then she stops. Silence. I pick up the snow globe Gram gave me and shake it. A flurry of snowflakes circles a mountain and falls around a family of skiers. A mother, a father, and one child.

"Oh… wow," says Raynee finally.

"Yeah," I say glumly. I turn the globe so all the snow piles into the sky, and the family hangs upside down.

"But your parents are great," she whispers. Her own parents are not so great. He drives a FedEx lorry, and when he's in town, which isn't all that often, he gives Raynee lots of presents. I guess that's good. But, we both agreed, it's kind of weird. He probably feels guilty. He'd taken both of us to the Stanford Mall plenty of times. And bought us expensive stuff that it was hard to say thank you for, because it was just too much. But in between?

Nothing. And her mom is super strict, to make up for her father being gone.

Suddenly, I want to talk. Now, with Raynee listening, I'm finally ready. "I need them," I say, right out, just like that. "They can't do this to me!" Whew. That feels good. And true.

Raynee considers this. I see her, lying on her bed just like I am, with one leg crossed over the other, pointing her toes at the ceiling. "Well, maybe they don't get that. Maybe it's because you're so, you know, kind of cheery. Ordinary. No problems. They think they can do what they want, and you'll be fine. Because you're always fine."

True. Mom brags all the time that I'm trouble-free. Even when I was a baby. No colic. No crying at night. Just smiling like a little Buddha. Not a great student, but a solid student. Average. No problems. Maybe that makes me the kind of kid who gets left. Not because I'm rotten, but because I'm not. If I had been more of a handful, maybe they'd have had to stay on top of me. Together in the same house, even.

"Yeah," I say, "maybe if I get myself in trouble, they'll realise they have to put aside their own stuff, and just kind of get united in helping me." Like when they see my report card. That might just do it.

"Uh-huh," she agrees, "you're just a kid. You've got to need them more."

I have to move. "You want to go for a run, girl?" I ask. I'm already fishing under my bed for my Nikes.

"No way," says Raynee promptly. "I'm gonna spend my day off watching 'Animal Planet'." Raynee wants to be a zoo veterinarian. That's almost like going to medical school; it's that hard. Good thing she's a better student than I am. Way better.

I fly downstairs and out the door. "Hey, Super Woman!" It's Mom. She's at the open door of her little VW Beetle. It's the colour of bright red lipstick. Part of her new (without Rashida) life.

"Gotta run! Gotta fly!" I say, not coming too close, jogging in place. She pushes the last box onto the seat.

"Hold on. I'll come too."

I stop my feet moving. "What? You never jog!" I say. Dad sometimes bikes with me when I run at the weekend. Mom, never. She always sleeps in. Dad and I tiptoe around in the dawn house, plugging in the coffee maker, so that the fresh scent wakes her up gradually. Then, out the door for a race with the rising sun. At the end, Dad and I stop at Jake's for sticky buns to take back for breakfast. I squeeze the OJ. He serves her in bed on a tray. We used to feel special, he and I, like we got a part of the day no one else did. And we were taking care of Mom together, like she was something precious we shared. But I suppose that hadn't mattered to her.

"First time for everything," she says. "Wait, I've got some trainers in here somewhere." She pulls a pair of canvas deck shoes from under the car seat.

"Mom, those aren't running shoes." I stare at her slim feet. "You don't even have socks. You'll get blisters."

She smiles. "Nah. I won't. I bet you have duct tape in your bum bag. You can sort me out! Come on," she coaxes. "I was always jealous of you and your dad, out there drinking in the sunshine."

My jaw drops. "You were?"

"Sure." She stands up. "Race you to Jake's!" She sprints hard, shoes slapping, down the street, not even bothering to warm up. She turns and waves, running backwards, hair in her eyes, shirt-tails flapping.

I start out loose, warming up the way Dad taught me. She's no longer in sight, and then there she is — waiting for me, waving.

"Hey, slowcoach," she calls. Out of breath already, of course.

"You've got to learn to pace yourself," I say, stopping beside her. She puts her arm around me, leaning.

"Good thing I've got such a strong, steady girl," she says.

I shake her off. "I'm not so strong. I'm not."

"Hey!" she says, surprised. She puts both hands on

my shoulders and turns me square towards her. "What is it, 'Shida-girl?"

I take a breath, surprised to find I'm trembling. "I messed up at school. Dad's gonna kill me."

"Huh," she says matter-of-factly. "Happens to the best of us. So what went wrong?" Suddenly I'm mad at her. She doesn't care. She thinks this is normal.

"What went wrong?" I repeat. "You did!" I'm yelling. "You went wrong. You!" I push her away. As I do, she reaches out and pulls the water bottle from my holder. She unscrews the top. I watch in disbelief. She's thirsty? Now? I feel hot tears spurt onto my face. She really doesn't care. How can she not be upset with me?

But she's holding it out to me. "Here," she says. "Go ahead. It will help, I promise."

I grab the bottle and dump it right over her head. It mats her hair and runs down into her shirt.

"Woo-eee," she yelps. Then, "Feel better?"

"No," I say. The water drips down inside her collar. I can't help but smile, just a little.

"Brrr," she says. Then she says softly, "I didn't know you were so mad, baby. I didn't know. I thought you were fine."

"Not fine," I say. "You're the one who's fine. With your bookshelves and red car! I'm not. Dad's not."

She takes my hand like I was a much younger

86

girl. "I see," she says. She thinks for a moment. I stand there, trying not to cry. "I know what we need," she decides, "First, sticky buns. Then home. Your father should be there by now."

When we see Dad standing on the porch, I have the white bakery bag smelling of cinnamon, but my face is blotchy and my eyes are puffy. Mom's hair is still matted and her shirt is wet and sticking to her.

"Rashida!" he calls. "I was worried. I came home and you weren't here!" He tries to look stern. "Leave me a note next time, okay? Where have you been?" He looks at Mom's wet shirt. "Swimming?"

"Jogging," I say.

"Huh," he says. He looks Mom up and down, taking in her raggedy shoes, and shakes his head.

She smiles, "Hey, there's a first time for everything."

Then he sees the bag in my hand. "Are those what I think they are?" he asks, pointing at it. We sit down on the top step. Me in the middle. Mom pokes me. "Rashida has something she wants to say," she says.

I don't want to. But I'd rather say it now than later. "I messed up at school," I whisper.

"And that's not all," says Mom when I don't go on. "Yeah, Rashida did one of her one-eighty turnarounds at school. But don't blame her. It's my fault."

Dad stops chewing and looks at me. "You mess up and it's Mom's fault?" he says. It sounds silly when he says it.

"That how it feels," I say stiffly. I turn to Mom. "It feels like – the course markers that are supposed to be there? I can't find them. Like my map's upside down, and my compass needle won't stop twirling."

Dad's moustache starts to do that bristling thing it does when he's losing his temper. "What does that mean?" he starts, but Mom nods and leans in. She's talking thoughtfully now, frowning and looking into the distance like she's telling a story.

"Remember that Windy Hill course we did in August?" She squints at me. "Remember?" she looks at Dad. "I'd have never done that without you, girl, never in a million years." She waits.

"Yeah, I know that," I say finally. "But I got us turned around."

"Sure, but we recovered. And it showed me I could do all kinds of things I'd never tried before. And now, seems like it's me who's got us all turned around." She stops, then goes on, carefully. "This is my first time on my own in years. And I don't want to do it without you. Don't know if I can, even. But I will try if I have to." She reaches across, touches Dad's hand and then mine. "It's not easy. Not for you two, not for me. But I need to be on my way. I know

I do. And that I'll be better for it. And so will we all. Eventually. But it hurts now. It's hard. Like we're at the top of that hill, finding out we were turned around. Remember? But when we looked back, we could see that marker. Being apart from you? That's the hardest. But I can look around and find you. Always. Here you are." She puts her hands to my face for a second. Then she goes on, "Right now, I'm with you. Here and now. But also tonight, when I'm across town. I'm still with you. You're where I point. Like I'm a compass needle, and you're my true North. Right, Hugh?"

He shakes his head, a little sad. "And I'm not going anywhere." He puts his hand on my neck for a moment. "I'm right here, 'Shida. Shoot, goes without saying." He leans back, embarrassed. "Shoot," he says again.

I don't dare to look into either of their faces. It's a new kind of snow-globe moment. Kind of sad, not just glad. We make our own little world inside the glass globe, even while life goes on outside, pulling us apart.

Mom will get in her shiny car and drive off. Dad and I will go to the parent conference by ourselves. Even though we've had this little talk, I know his moustache will do its bristly thing. He wouldn't be Dad without that. I'll have to start again at school and get it right. We will get through it, because really, we're all right here, the three of us in this together.

I turn to Mom. "A compass needle has two ends. It can point two ways at once." And, to show them, I put an arm around each of them.

"Woo-ee," says Mom softly. "How'd you get so clever?"

Dad shakes his head, "A clever girl wouldn't have messed up at school," he says. But he holds my hand hard.

"That's book-clever," says Mom. "I think what we've got here is something different. We've got a heart-clever gal."

"Best kind," says Dad. "The very best kind."

I close my eyes, and freeze the moment for my snow globe. I shake it, to see what happens. The three of us sit on the porch and flakes of cinnamon and autumn leaves float around our heads and shoulders. Now that I've got that scene in one of my globes, I think I can hold on.

Broken Flower-Heads

KATE PETTY

O K. So here's an example of one of my mum's irritating little habits. She rescues flower-heads if they break off when Dad is mowing the lawn, or even if she finds one in the street. She brings it home and puts it in an eggcup of water. Nought out of ten for flower-arranging. Just a windowsill full of eggcups containing manky, short-stemmed flowers. She rescues spiders, too, instead of stamping on them like any sensible person. And wasps. Outside a French café, once, she tipped out a whole beer glass of drowning wasps – set them free again to have their evil way. The other customers were outraged. I've never disowned anyone so quickly.

I don't know what it is – we got on fine when I was little, but these days, everything about my mum is annoying. She's got a big bottom, for a start. It's always there. In fact, she's always there. Most of the time, I just want to tell her to butt out – to stay away from me and my friends when we're at home. To stop telling me how to wear my hair. To let me decide if it's cold enough to wear a jacket. I had a go at her about it last night – asked her to get off my back – but it never works. She shouts at first, but then her eyes just fill with tears and Dad comes along and gets angry with me for upsetting her. It's pathetic. Why doesn't he get angry with *her* for upsetting *me?* It's not fair.

And she faffs about. When we're all in a hurry, Dad revving the car engine impatiently, where's Mum? Still getting dressed! She blames her arthritis. Says she can't do fiddly things. I couldn't admit to any of my friends that my mum has arthritis. It makes her sound senile – and she's barely fifty.

Every night, I end up writing in my diary: "Must try to be nicer to Mum." I know I should, but I just can't stand her a lot of the time.

My grandma lives round the corner. Mum is always trying to get us to drop in on her. I only have to be walking to the shops to meet my friends, and Mum says, "Why don't you drop in on Grandma on the way home? You know how she loves to see you." But it's always the last thing I want to do on my way home, because I've usually stayed with my friends as long as possible and I'm late for supper, homework – whatever. Especially recently, because we quite often bump into some lads from school in town. And I think Sean Young is quite interested in me. Mum frets about Grandma even more since she had a minor heart attack, but she seems OK to me.

❧ ❧ ❧

I was wrong about Grandma. She isn't OK. This morning, Saturday, there was a knock on the door. Dad was taking my younger brother to football, and I assumed Mum would open the door. But she didn't, and the knocking went on, so I went down to open it in my dressing-gown. Two people in uniform stood on the doorstep: a policewoman and a paramedic. "Is your mother here?" they asked.

"MUM!" I yelled up the stairs, and Mum poked her head round the bathroom door. She was wrapped in a towel. How embarrassing. She saw the man and the woman. "Oh!" she said. "What is it?"

"It's about your mother," said the policewoman. "Would you like me to come upstairs to talk to you?"

"Oh," said Mum. "No, wait there. I'll just slip a dressing-gown on." We waited. Eventually Mum came downstairs in her dressing-gown. Nothing underneath it. Gross.

"I'm afraid your mother has had a fall in the street, Mrs Blaise. The ambulance has taken her to hospital. A neighbour called us. They told us where you lived. We'll take you with us to the hospital."

"Is – is she all right?" asked my mother. (Duh! Would they be here if she was?)

"We think you should get to the hospital as quickly as possible," was all they would say. So Mum rushed upstairs to get dressed while I entertained the man and the woman as best as I could. We talked about the weather and how fond of my granny I must be, etc, etc. And Mum didn't emerge.

I went upstairs. "Mum!" I hissed. "They're waiting for you." I poked my head round the door. There was Mum in her knickers and she was trying to do her bra up at the back.

"I can't do my bra up, darling," she said. "My fingers just won't work. Would you do it for me?"

"Oh, for God's sake, Mum!" But I did it for her, trying not to look, and then legged it downstairs again. "She won't be long," I said, and Mum appeared a few minutes later, looking more or less OK. She went off with them, asking me to ring Dad on his mobile and let him know what's going on. "All right!" I said. "Just go, will you?"

❦ ❦ ❦

Grandma died. Grandma is dead! I can't believe it. A few minutes after Dad got back there was a telephone call. I let him answer it – people I want to speak to only ever call my mobile. And I heard him saying, "I see. I see," over and over again. Then he came and found me, and put on his caring expression.

"She's died, hasn't she?" I said, before he could go into the whole rigmarole of explaining.

"Poor Mum," he said. "My poor little Linda." (That's Mum's name.) "I'm going to see her at the hospital. I'll ask Eddie's friends to hang on to him after football, but I'd like you to wait here, darling, and be on phone duty."

I scowled.

"Darling! Have a heart!"

"All right. OK!"

I sat there, waiting. It was funny, Dad saying, "My poor little Linda." I could have sworn he was going to say, "My poor little Lucy." (That's my name.) I don't think of Mum as little. Ever. But I suppose she was once. A little girl with a mummy, and then a teenager, like me. And now she hasn't got a mummy anymore. Weird.

When they came home, Dad had his arm tightly round Mum's shoulders. She was very tear-stained.

"I'm sorry about Grandma," I said. "Can I go out now?"

❦ ❦ ❦

Dad took the next few days off work to help with organising the funeral. Mum's sister Denise came to stay. Luckily she left my extremely wet cousin, Laura, behind. I was very happy to go to school and get away from all the moping, but apparently Laura really,

really wanted to come and help with the funeral preparations. What did she think it was, a wedding?

One evening, Auntie Denise asked me to go over to Grandma's house with her – to help her clear out the fridge, and so on. I didn't want to, but everyone else seemed to think it was a perfectly reasonable request, so off we went. It was strange, letting ourselves into the empty house. I couldn't believe Grandma wasn't just going to pop up somewhere. Denise sat down heavily at one point. She had a weep. "I don't have a mother any more," she said, blowing her nose. "You never believe that day will come, Lucy. Mothers are just meant to be there, aren't they?"

"Huh," I said, but anything I might have added stuck in my throat, because my gaze suddenly fell on the windowsill, where there was a blowsy pink rose that must have broken off its stem, sitting in an eggcup of water. It was still pink and blossoming and alive, when Grandma wasn't. I didn't know she rescued flower-heads too.

We emptied the fridge. All those little things she kept. Just like Mum. Denise gave me a hug. I didn't really want one. I wasn't feeling as upset as she was.

🦋 🦋 🦋

Don't ever get involved in a funeral. They are a complete nightmare.

Mum, Dad and Denise spent the next three days

planning and organising and phoning. That's because no one in our family is a Christian, so they couldn't have it in a church, like normal people. They had to make up their own service for the crematorium. (The very word makes me want to run a mile.) So as well as sorting out flowers and hearses and coffins and tea and sandwiches for afterwards, they were trying to dredge up every detail of Grandma's life and going through the CDs, choosing the music she would have liked. They almost seemed to be enjoying themselves at times. Laughing. Me and my brother came home from school, made ourselves peanut-butter sandwiches and barely got a look-in.

Not, that is, until Mum had the bright idea that one of the grandchildren should stand up at the funeral and show off in some way or other. "Don't even think of asking me to play my flute in front of people," I warned before they got carried away.

Auntie Denise winked at Mum before saying: "Not even one of those duets you used to play with your mum? You know how thrilled Grandma was at the flute-playing tradition being carried on…" She giggled.

Mum could see that I was confused by them joking about the funeral. "It's all right, darling. Auntie Denise is teasing you. Always jealous of our music thing, weren't you, Denny?" I felt more confused than ever. "I just thought you might want to be part of it all, Lucy, and read a poem or something," she explained. "For Grandma."

"No way!" I grumbled. Now they really were joking.

"OK, OK," she said. "Wouldn't want to push you or anything." But I could see I had disappointed her.

"I'm sure Laura would love to do something," said Auntie Denise into the brief silence. "Shall I give her a ring?" I left them to their weird sense of humour and went off to watch telly.

🦋 🦋 🦋

The night before the funeral, Dad was printing off the order-of-service sheets. I went into his study, where the computer was. It smelt nice, of hot paper. "How are you doing, love?" he asked me, reaching out an arm to put round my waist. "Soon be over. Once we've had the funeral we can all get on with our lives. It will be tough for Mum, but we'll all help her, won't we?" He hugged me. "I suppose one day it will be you doing this for us. That's a strange thought, isn't it?"

"Da-ad! Weirdo." Funerals do peculiar things to people. I wish he hadn't said that, though. I felt very morbid for a bit. What if something happened to Mum and Dad − like a car accident or something? Eddie and I would have to live on peanut-butter sandwiches forever.

The next morning was a bit like before a

wedding. We all got dressed in our smart clothes. Flowers kept arriving. Not long before the hearse and the black saloons arrived, my uncle Mac and cousin Laura (the wet one) appeared. Laura looked annoyingly cool in some boots that were exactly the same as the ones I'd been coveting for ages. She ran up to Auntie Denise and threw her arms round her. "Mum, Mum…" I heard her cry into Denise's chest. "Mum – I've really, really missed you."

Funny, that. I've quite missed my mum over the last few days, too.

Then the cars arrived. We loaded the flowers that had been piling up outside the house onto Grandma's coffin. It was rather a small coffin. I couldn't believe that Grandma's dead body was actually inside it. Creepy. Then we got into the posh black cars with tinted windows and followed the hearse at a snail's pace to the crematorium.

And then everyone was sitting in the crematorium, listening to one of Grandma's favourite flute sonatas and blubbing. The music got to me, too. One by one, my relations stood up and said something about Grandma – quite interesting things, actually. Apparently she was a smasher when she was a girl (Great-Uncle Eric) and really quite stroppy (Great-Uncle Will), not unlike her elder daughter…

I thought he was referring to me at first, and I

looked around to see if people were staring at me, but they meant that Mum had been a stroppy teenager too. Must run in the family.

Tears were streaming down Laura's cheeks so fast that the poem she stumbled through was unintelligible. She definitely hadn't inherited the stroppy gene. For a moment there, I felt quite proud that I had. Via Mum. Huh. I looked at the two sisters – Mum and Auntie Denise – in the row in front. Mum is dark, like me, and Denny is blonde, like Laura. Grandma was dark when she was young. I wondered how it must feel when your daughter starts to turn out like you, and whether it's odd to have a fair child when you are dark, and vice versa. I think I want my children to be dark.

The last person to speak was Mum. She stood up there, cool and calm, not tearful at all. She was practically smiling. "I want to tell you about the wonderful, maddening, extraordinary person who was my mother…" she began. *Just like someone else I know*, I thought.

It was a huge relief to get outside after the service, and leave Grandma, in her coffin, behind. It was cool being driven back in the posh black cars, at a proper speed, too. We probably looked like film stars. Even Laura.

Our house was already full of people when we

got back, and you wouldn't believe how quickly it turned into a regular party, with beer and wine and everything. Eddie laid into the cider and soon conked out on the sofa. Great-Uncle Will cornered me about then.

"It's Lucy, isn't it?" he said, puffing terrible pipe smoke into my face. He must be almost the last pipe-smoker on the planet. "My, how you've grown up since I last saw you." I fixed a reasonably polite grin onto my face. "Still playing the flute, are you? Like my sister?"

"Yes," I said, in what I hoped was a conversational tone. I couldn't think of anything else to say, not that I needed to when faced with a garrulous, pipe-smoking old relative. I could safely leave the talking to him.

He laughed at me. "Just like your mother!" he guffawed. "Always the silent niece! She used to look at me in just that tone of voice!"

"Don't you mean – "

"Old joke, my dear. You have to indulge the old man. Just like your mother, you are, and just like my poor dear sister, God rest her soul. And perhaps you could get me another glass of this? Look out for George and Miranda on the way, will you? They're bringing my newest grandson with them."

I moved off quickly with his glass, keeping an eye

open for Mum's cousin George, possibly my favourite relation. Laura and I were bridesmaids when he married Miranda a few years ago, and now they have a divine baby. It wasn't hard to find them. They were in the centre of a circle formed by most of the people in the room, all cooing and gurgling at little Dino (how cute is that?) who was bobbing and smiling in his mother's arms and generally wowing the crowd.

George saw me crossing the room. "Lucy!" he called. "Come and meet my bonny, bonny boy!"

"Get my drink first!" called Great-Uncle Will.

"Yes, do that," said George, "and then come and have a cuddle. He doesn't bite. Yet!"

I refilled Great-Uncle Will's glass for him and then went over to the little family group. "Sit yourself down," said George, "and then I'll hand him over. Co-ome here, little fellow, come to Daddy."

"He's completely besotted!" said Miranda, handing Dino to George. "You've never seen such a doting daddy."

George placed Dino in my arms. I'd never held such a small baby before. Such a gentle little thing. He looked up at me trustingly and rested his tiny velvet hand on my wrist. "He'll act quizzical for a bit," said George, "but then he'll smile – and my boy smiles for England. Don't you, Dino?" And when

Dino did smile that wide, gummy smile I just wanted to love and protect him forever. "It's called being smitten," said George quietly in my ear. "Great, isn't it? Parenthood rocks, and don't let anyone tell you otherwise."

"Just wait till they turn into teenagers," said Aunty Denise, coming to join us. "Bit of a different story then."

"Denny!" said Mum arriving with two full glasses in her hand. "Don't put the poor boy off. Anyway," she stroked my hair and I couldn't shake her hand off because I didn't want to disturb Dino – "teenagers have their good moments too."

I started to seethe at her glib comments, but Dino smiled at me again. I suppose Mum held me like this. And wanted to love and protect me forever. So I put my anger to one side a little. "Was I like this once, Mum?" I asked her.

"Even more beautiful," she said. "Sorry, George and Miranda – I know you don't think it's possible – but Lucy was the most beautiful little baby girl you've ever seen."

"You were, actually," conceded George. "Still are, of course," he added.

Laura was suddenly there too. "Oi, what about me?" she said. "I was beautiful too, wasn't I, Mum?"

"Started something here, haven't you?" said Auntie

Denise to George, laughing. "All babies are beautiful," she said, "especially to their parents. Which is a good thing really. But maybe now is the time for a toast to Grandma, our darling mum, who loved us all, and who is with us now, I'm sure. To Mum," and she raised her glass.

"To Mum, Grandma, Ellen, Auntie, my dear sister," came the response from round the room.

Everyone left soon after that. We felt a bit flat, to tell you the truth, just Mum, Dad, Eddie and me, and quite a lot of clearing-up to do. It was getting dark, and I saw Mum standing, looking out of the window at the garden. I crossed the room and gave her a hug. "Love you, Mum."

"Thank you, darling," she said.

Dad was still washing glasses. "Take those last bottles out to the recycling box, would you, Lucy? It's out the front – they'll be collecting them tomorrow."

I took the bottles out to the green box by the front gate. A blackbird sang in the hawthorn tree. I had the absurd thought that it was Grandma. Where the flowers had been stacked up by the front door, a few flower-heads that had been broken off lay glowing in the twilight. Four of them. I picked them up.

Back in the kitchen, I took an eggcup from the cupboard, filled it with water and put the flowers in it.

Barn Swallows

AMY BOESKY

It was my fault they fell. My mother opened the door, but I was the one who begged her to. If it hadn't been for me, they'd still be safe.

What I remember most clearly about that summer, after I finished fifth grade, was that my mother suddenly seemed different to me. Her expression was darker, her habits sharpened. She was the same woman in theory, but now she was all edges, the softness gone. With my younger sister Sarah, who was only eight, she was more or less the same. But not with me. I would be starting middle school in the autumn – in our town, the middle school was more or less attached to the high school, only a few dozen yards of tarmac between them. That meant I had to take more responsibility (my mother's phrase). All of a sudden, we were at odds, my mother and I. It felt to me like the music had changed in the middle of a dance. She and I were no longer in step – just a tiny beat off and always missing each other. If I was reading, she wanted help with folding laundry. If I felt like baking, she had just cleaned the kitchen. My music bothered her. When the phone was for me, her mouth set. I knew I was annoying her, and that saddened me, but what was much worse was how much she was annoying me. Her voice, which I used to love, now sounded flat and common. The stories she told seemed small and pointless. Worst of all, I had learned things at school that she didn't know. For a long time I'd believed that she knew everything, and now I knew that wasn't true.

I'd had a new teacher for fifth grade, Ms Tilbury, who had transferred to rural Vermont from Boston. She dressed differently and talked differently from the people in our town, and she always seemed excited, as if something amazing were about to happen. Sometimes I dreamed that she was my real mother and my own parents were just taking care of me for the time being. That was one of a number of things I liked pretending. Other times I imagined that Ms Tilbury would invite me to move to Boston with her and I would shyly say yes and I would leave Vermont and never come back. Ms Tilbury lived in town in a creamy Victorian house with window-boxes. Morgan Dickinson had been to her house once, to drop off a homework assignment, and she said the entire front room – the room most people would have used as a living room – was crammed with books. Ms Tilbury knew everything: the population of Sri Lanka, how igneous rocks formed, ten different species of lichen, the names of every bone in the human hand, and the way a verb behaved in a sentence. When she didn't know something right off the top of her head, she would say, "Let's look it up!" as if that were a wonderful prospect.

At first when I brought home stories about Ms Tilbury – back before everything changed – my mother hung on every word, like she was learning with me – like she hadn't already BEEN a fifth-grader, all those years ago! – but after a while she seemed to get tired of Ms Tilbury stories. Then one day, a few weeks before the winter break in December, Mandy Richards announced that she was going to Boston at the weekend to see *The Nutcracker*. "What's that?" I asked, and Mandy laughed. Ms Tilbury stuck up for me by turning Mandy's attention towards something else. She tried to, anyway. She asked the class if anyone else knew *The Nutcracker* and pretty much everyone did, except the Morgan boys (who never know anything) and me. I could feel my face burning the whole time that Ms Tilbury talked about the ballet, and Russian composers, and the story of the little wooden nutcracker who came to life and danced with Clara.

When my mother asked me how school was that day, I wouldn't answer. There were so many different feelings swirling around in me — shame and embarrassment and anger — and at the same time, a bitter-tasting sense that I didn't want my mother to know what had happened. What if my mother had never heard of the ballet, either? I couldn't have stood that. It was better to keep it to myself.

So after that day, there were things that I didn't mention at home. I didn't tell my mother that I won a prize for an essay I wrote about the human body. We each had a body part assigned to us — mine was the inner ear — and I wrote a detailed essay about the labyrinthine structures inside it and the hairs that moved sound vibrations along the miniature channels. Oscillations. That was the word for it. Ms Tilbury gave me a dictionary with my name embossed on the front in gold, but I didn't show it to my mother. I brought it home in my schoolbag and kept it under my bed, and sometimes at night when I couldn't sleep I would take out my torch and shine its sallow light on a word I didn't know: "prognosticate" — to predict the future. "Pandemonium" — a form of chaos. One day (I "prognosticated"), I would know more words than my mother knew. The bitter taste in my mouth came back, and it was hard to fall asleep.

The morning of the swallows, I'd been begging my mother to open the barn so my sister Sarah and I could play college in the front room. The more I wheedled, the more stuff she had to do – putting the laundry in and making phone calls and lifting the wet things out of the washing machine and stuffing them into the dryer and then making yet another phone call, and all the while the sun blazed overhead and my eyes burned with the heat. I could smell the dampness of the barn's interior, cool and murky and cobwebby, but I knew that if I asked her one more time she'd accuse me of whining. So I waited.

I trailed after her, trying to stay just enough out of her way not to irritate her but close enough that she wouldn't forget. Mr Graber, who owned the place before we did, had kept a real shop in the front room, and there were still remnants of things lying on the shelves – old hinges and mildewy wooden signs and syrup buckets and a few stray farm tools, and there was a school desk set up in one corner that nobody had ever cleaned, not for about twenty years or so. Once, Sarah had found a petrified slab of birthday cake in one of the drawers. We loved playing there. Now that it was July, smack in the middle of the summer, with school so far away from us on either side that it seemed pretty much impossible that there'd ever be anything required of us again, the shop was a refuge – a cool, dim room to hide in. A room where we could hide inside the things that we made up. In the game I liked best, I was a teacher and Sarah my student, abject and adoring, and I sat at the ancient school desk and showed off my new-found words to her while she fidgeted. Prevaricate. Palindrome. But we needed the barn door opened first.

"OK, OK," my mother said, rubbing gunk off her hands and looking irritated. We were in the way of what she needed to get done, that's why she sounded that way. She had her daytime voice, which was all business and edge, and her night-time voice, when she read to us from one of the books she'd saved from when she was young. I loved those times the best. But we needed her now. The barn door was eight feet high, with a wooden bolt keeping it closed, and even she had to pull a milk crate over and stand on her tiptoes to slide it back. It stuck a little, and she had to lean into it with all her might – she wasn't very tall – and then she made a little sucking sound, the breath coming out of her in a spurt. The door yanked back as a skein of straw fell on the grass at our feet.

"Look," Sarah breathed, her eyes bulging as she dropped to her knees on the grass, her index finger pointing.

Three baby swallows had spilled out, caught in

varying positions of fright and struggle. The nest had been tucked between the barn and the door, and when my mother tugged at the door, it tumbled free. We couldn't see the birds' mother anywhere – not on the telephone wire behind us, not on the gutter of the barn roof, not across the road on Mr Graber's old rotting sign. The babies looked sticky and transparent to me, lying in triple silhouette on the dry grass like a prehistoric painting of flight. My mother shaded her eyes with her hand, looking down at them, and for what seemed like ages, none of us spoke.

"The mother won't come back now that we're here," I announced. "Ms Tilbury told us."

My mother looked doubtful, but I stood my ground. "We have to take care of them now," I said. The way I looked at her, what I meant was: *You have to. You have to make this right. It's your fault, and you have to fix it.*

My mother straightened up. "Sarah, there's a shoebox upstairs in my closet, on the shelf where I keep winter things. Can you bring it to me?"

Sarah ran off and then back again, red in the face and huffing. The box looked ancient and one side was a little torn.

We lined it with grass and twigs, and we used my mother's old rubber spatula to winch the swallow babies in. Their eyes were moving under tight-closed lids. Sarah touched one gingerly, her finger trembling.

I touched, too. The littlest one's body stuck to my finger and its mouth opened and closed. Its skin felt like membrane. Like the canal inside the ear.

"They're thirsty," I said judiciously, squinting up at the bright sun. "They need water."

For the next half hour, Sarah and I dripped water on the baby birds with an eyedropper while my mother went inside to make some phone calls. When she came back she had a determined look on her face. "Hold the box carefully," she told me. "We're taking them to VINS."

VINS (it stood for the Vermont Institute of Natural Science) had a building a few miles from us called the Raptor Centre where injured birds were nursed back to health. It was a place we went only rarely, when our cousins came to visit, and I was amazed my mother would consider this now. She always had so much to do around the house. But she had taken this on as a project, and I could tell she wasn't going to stop now. It was as if more than these baby birds was at stake. Maybe she wanted to show me that she knew how to make it better.

We climbed into the van. I sat in the front – a new privilege, it still felt strange to me – with the cardboard box resting lightly on my lap. I tried to hold it perfectly still over the bumps. The babies looked flatter and their colour seemed to be darkening. They looked like little hearts – raw, beef-colored, translucent. With each jolt of the road, they pulsed and twitched.

We tried two entrances at VINS before we found the small room at the back marked "Hospital". A woman named Lindsey came out to help us. Her hair hung down her back in a long braid. She frowned when she saw the birds. "They're only a few days old," she said, slipping her hand into the box and gently lifting them out. "They're cold," she added, rubbing them dexterously with her fingers, and as she touched them we could see that they were trembling. I thought I heard an accusation in her voice. I remembered all the water I'd dripped on them and bit my lip.

But as I looked around me, I felt relief. They could fix birds here. Any kind of birds, even the giant raptors with wings shot off or the hawks that collided with cars. They had everything: birdfood, cages, medical supplies… Surely they could deal with three tiny barn swallows. Lindsey was explaining to my mother that the birds were dehydrated and she was going to give them each a shot. I had that feeling I'd had all last year in Ms Tilbury's classroom:

everything here was clean, organised, official. Lindsey and her hospital would make it right.

But what I heard next made my heart fall.

"We can't keep them, though," Lindsey said. "Not barn swallows. We're really only set up for raptors – hawks, owls…" She was talking to my mother, not to us. "The best thing would be to try to find other nests in your barn – but you need to find ones that have babies about the same age. Put one in each nest. If you don't overload it, the mother might adopt the new one."

Might. I didn't look at the swallows.

I thought about oscillation: how sound moves through the ear. One word after another. *We can't keep them, though. Not barn swallows.*

Lindsey kept stroking the smallest bird, who was starting to look a little fluffier. "It's probably the best thing – now," she said. My mother asked some questions and wrote some things down on the pad of paper she kept in her handbag. She looked pretty worried. As we were leaving Lindsey told us, "If it ever happens again, just leave the birds alone. It's a myth, that argument that the mother won't come back. They usually do."

My mother glanced at me, surprised. Something flashed in her eyes but she didn't say anything.

"But Ms Tilbury said – " Sarah began.

I grabbed her arm. "Let's go," I said.

The little sign that said "Hospital" swung back and forth as I clambered back into the van, balancing the box on my lap. I felt betrayed. What was the good of all that information? How helpful was it to tell us to take these poor swallows back and peel them off of each other, one by one, and stuff them into other nests to perish?

I'd been wrong, and it was my fault that they were going to die. There was no word in my dictionary for what I was feeling.

None of us said much on the ride home. I kept staring down at the baby birds, a million things crowding into my head. Had Ms Tilbury really told me that, or had I just wanted to say she had? Because I didn't want my mother to be right.

It felt quicker driving back. All too soon we were pulling up in front of the barn, the door gaping open.

My mother took the torch down from its hook just inside the store room. I couldn't even look inside or think about playing anything anymore. I was tired of making things up.

We scoured the barn for swallows' nests. We found a few way up in the eaves, but they were all empty. Right at the back of the barn, we found one with some birds inside, but they looked big – my mother thought they were weeks older than ours. She didn't like the thought of slipping any of ours inside. "The others would get all the food," she said. She shook her head. "I can't see it."

"Anyway, we can't separate them," she added, speaking the exact words that were burning inside my heart.

I glanced at her, then away. I felt exactly the way she did. I couldn't bear to separate them.

"Maybe the mother will still come back if we leave them all together in their box," Sarah said hopefully.

We agreed it was the best strategy. But we couldn't leave them in the old shoebox, and their nest was destroyed.

"Let's try to make a nest," my mother said.

"Make a nest?" I repeated incredulously.

She didn't look at me.

"Sarah," she said calmly. "See if you can find my old wicker basket. The one I used to keep sewing in. I think it's in the cellar." She turned to me. "Annie, let's get some straw and grass."

We spent ages on that basket. Sarah and I lined it with the softest grass we could find. The hardest part was getting it back up where the old nest had been. My mother bent wire from a hanger to make a hook, but even so there was nothing to hang it from. She told us that she wanted to be able to lift it down so she could check on the birds. At last she rigged something together that she thought might work. Propping a ladder against the side of the barn, she climbed up and balanced the basket where the original nest had been. "OK," she said at last, wiping her face with her shirt. "That ought to work."

I stared at the wicker basket, dangling awkwardly from its hook. I felt like she was playing at something, the way earlier in the day I had wanted to play at college. I was angry and I didn't know why.

"Annie," my mother said, her voice low. "We've tried everything we could."

She was letting me off the hook and it made me even angrier. I got up without a word and scoured the sky but there was no sign of the mother swallow. Only the flimsy wicker nest my mother had made. I knew then, as sure as I've ever known anything, that the baby birds were going to die.

She went back in the house, and after a while Sarah did too. But I couldn't. I staked out a position a few dozen yards away, and with my dad's old binoculars clenched in my sweaty hands, I waited for what seemed like forever. I stayed crouched in the long grass until the light faded and the first stars came out. Finally, my legs aching, I crossed back to the house, where I could see the light shining on the screen porch. My mother was reading to Sarah, her voice slow and halting. She didn't read aloud beautifully, the way Ms Tilbury did. She didn't have as many words. Maybe she didn't even know what *The Nutcracker* was. But I didn't care about that anymore. I could see her silhouette through the screens, her hands turning the pages, her hair falling across her face, and suddenly I felt like crying. I realised then that my mother did not know the answers to everything. There were problems she couldn't fix. But at the same time, I understood that she knew things nobody else knew. Her hands, lifting the pages of Sarah's book. Her eyes, turning back to search for me in the darkness. She never complained that I had misquoted Ms Tilbury. She never blamed me for what happened to the barn swallows. She knew so much more than I could possibly fathom. And what I knew now was this: when I crossed back into the brightness of the porch, she would be there, waiting for me.

Not Just a Pretty Face

JEAN URE

When my mum was young, she won a beauty contest – "Queen of the South Coast". There is a picture of her (Dad had it framed and hung on the wall) in a swimming costume: black, one-piece. She's holding up a silver cup and has a kind of spiky crown stuck on her head, to show that she's the winner. Her hair is a bright, foaming red, her eyes are green, like sea water, and she's giving one of those big, mouth-stretching smiles at the camera, showing all her teeth. She looks totally drop-dead gorgeous.

I personally happen to think that beauty contests are degrading. Wild horses wouldn't get me to put on a swimsuit and parade up and down in front of a load of gawkers. No way!

But that's just me. The rest of my family do not agree. I once said to Mum that I thought it was very belittling for women to behave this way, but Mum just laughed and said, "Oh, nobody took it seriously! It was a bit of fun, that's all."

I said, "It's not all. It's demeaning. It turns women into sex objects."

"Rubbish!" said Dad. "Don't you give me any of that feminist guff!"

Dad's not really as Stone Age as that makes him sound; he just enjoys teasing me. But at the same time, he is hugely proud of Mum, which is why he insists on having her picture on the wall. Every now and again, Mum takes it down and hides it away somewhere, but Dad always notices and makes her put it back up. I suppose it's quite touching, in a way — I mean, after all those years of being married. On the other hand, I do find it seriously annoying when he defends things like beauty contests. I always rise to the bait! I just can't seem to help it. I guess I used to go on a bit — "getting on her soap box", as one of my grans calls it. Not that that was any reason for Jack to insult me. He's always insulting me. It makes me so angry!

"I'm entitled to my opinions," I said.

"Yeah? Well, you'd just better watch it," Jack replied. "If you're not careful, you'll turn into some withered old sour-faced stick that no man'll look twice at."

Honestly. Brothers! Talk about sexist. I opened my mouth to retort that it didn't bother me one little bit whether men looked twice at me, it didn't even bother me if they didn't look once; but Dad got in first and said, quite sharply, "That's quite enough of that, young man! There's no need to get personal."

Mum, reproachfully, said, "Jack, that's not worthy!"

Jack had the grace to look a bit ashamed, but instead of apologising, which he ought to have done, he just muttered about "sour grapes" and went banging out of the room.

"Idiot!" I yelled.

"Oh, Kira, sweetheart!" Mum hugged me to her. She's a very touchy-feely kind of person. "Try to take no notice… he's at that age."

He was fourteen; two years older than me. What's so special about that? Just because you're fourteen it means you can be rude and hurtful to people?

I knew why he'd done it: he wouldn't ever hear any criticism of Mum. Not that I had been criticising. Not Mum personally. Things were probably different in Mum's day; she probably hadn't known any better. But Jack was almost more besotted than Dad. He just loved having a mum he could show off to all his friends. I'd watched him do it. Totally sickening. And, of course, he looks just like her. Wouldn't you know?

Me, I take after Dad. Dad is actually quite

fanciable – well, my best friend Emma seems to think so – but what looks good on a man doesn't necessarily look good on a girl. I knew I couldn't ever compete with Mum, 'cos I'd heard people say so – grans and grandads, and elderly aunties, when they hadn't realised I was squatting under the table or skulking behind the sofa, with my ears flapping.

"Such a pity!" (That all Mum's looks had gone to Jack, and none to me.) "It's so much more important for a girl."

"Not that she isn't quite prettyish – "

"Oh, but she'll never compete with her mum!"

I didn't want to compete with Mum. I just wanted to be left alone in peace to be me, which meant not being constantly reminded that Mum was the family beauty and that Jack took after her and that I was only "quite prettyish". Actually, they didn't even think I was prettyish anymore. I'd seen to that! I mean, I ask you, who wants to be prettyish? Yeeurgh! Not me.

I knew it upset Mum when I went around looking what she called "deliberately ugly".

"You're an attractive girl! Why do you do this to yourself?"

Maybe that was why I did it – because I wanted to upset her. If so, how mean can you be? But it just gets me so angry! All this rubbish about "looks are important" and "make the most of yourself".

Mum particularly hated the dungarees that I'd found in a charity shop. And the big boots that went with them – "clumping", she said they were – and the grungy grey vest that looked like it had been fished out of a thousand-year-old sewer. Smelt like it sometimes, too. I told Mum that I did it to feel comfortable. "I'm trying to express the essential me."

Mum was really good about it, I've got to admit. She sighed, but she let me do my own thing. She never nagged. In some ways, it might almost have been better if she had, 'cos then I could have got on my high horse and had, like, a slanging match, which was what Emma quite often did with her mum when her mum objected to what she was wearing. I think maybe a bit of a shout-about might have, sort of... I dunno! Got it out of my system, or something. Like it would have been a relief, now and again, to bellow and bawl and accuse Mum of being a tyrant. "You're so unfair. You're so unreasonable."

But Mum has always been determinedly understanding. Unlike my grans and grandads! Both sets. They thought it was terrible, me going around "like something off a building site". You can't really bellow and bawl at your grandparents, so I just used to swagger and make like they were so ancient and out of it they had no idea what it was cool for kids to wear. And then, when they started to get a bit uppity and ruffled, and mutter about my attitude and "taking that tone of voice", Mum would always step in and come to my defence.

"It's just a phase she's going through… she'll grow out of it."

I think she must have told Dad to lay off me, 'cos he just used to look and shake his head, but never actually said anything. Jack, needless to say, sided with the ancients. He said I was a sight and that I needn't think he was going to introduce me to any of his friends, but I had no desire to be introduced to any of his friends, so that didn't bother me. I wasn't interested in boys! Well, that is what I told myself. It's what I told Emma, too.

"Boys are rubbish! They've only got one thing on their mind."

"Yeah, right," said Emma. "Football. Yuck!"

Actually, I hadn't meant football, I'd meant the male obsession with the way girls look. I'd heard Jack and his mates talking about the girls in their class. Some of the things they said were just so horrid. Like, for instance, there was this one girl that was fat, so they called her Porker, and kept making piggy noises, snorting and honking and rolling about with coarse laughter. Then there was one they said was so ugly, you'd turn to stone if you looked at her, and one they all said they wouldn't "touch with a bargepole".

"They never even think they might be clever, or funny, or —"

"Or kind," said Emma.

"Or just nice people. All they care about is whether they're pretty."

"Yeah, like, does it really matter?" said Emma. And then she splayed her fingers and said, "Look, d'you like my nails?" She'd gone and painted them bright blue, with little silver stars.

"How long did that take?" I shrieked.

Emma giggled and said, "All evening!"

"You spent all evening just making your nails look pretty?"

Emma said, "Yes!" and giggled again. And then she must have realised that there was a bit of a contradiction here, 'cos she turned kind of pinkish and muttered, "I didn't do it to make them look pretty, I did it... to be creative!" She waggled her fingers triumphantly. "It's modern art, see? You could do it to yours, then we could go and be on display somewhere."

I didn't want to be on display. I thought it was demeaning. And I certainly wasn't going to paint my nails with silver stars. No way! I couldn't have, in any case; I'd chewed all my nails right down to the quick. It was what Emma would have done if she was really serious, but she obviously wasn't. She'd fallen into the same trap as all the rest of them. Looks were everything! Needless to say, she hotly denied it – "I am so not interested in the way I look!" And by way of proving it she ruffled up her hair and made her eyes cross and stuck her tongue out. "See?"

Next day, when she came into school, I noticed she'd removed all the varnish from her nails. All the little silver stars had gone, which she claimed was "just to show you", though more likely our class teacher, Mrs Meeks, had got at her. Mrs Meeks is very plain and wholesome. She goes in for cardigans and flat shoes and she once went ballistic when Laura Brigstock showed up with a stud in her nose. I like Mrs Meeks; I don't think Laura Brigstock had any right to call her a frumpy old bag. I said this to Emma, and Emma said, "Well, but it's her own fault… People don't have to go round looking like a sack of potatoes."

You see what I mean about Emma not being serious? Although she is my best friend in all the world, she really has no principles whatsoever. She cannot be relied upon. We had a good demonstration of this the following week, when it was Open Day, with parents descending upon the school in hordes. My mum and dad were there, and so were Emma's. Mum, as usual, was looking what Dad calls "Knock 'em in the aisles". His way of saying drop-dead gorgeous. It was something that just seemed to come naturally to her. I couldn't really accuse her of spending hours painting her nails or doing up her face, though she did buy a lot of clothes. Dad loved to see Mum buy clothes, he always encouraged her. "Go on!" he'd say, if Mum was hesitating. "Hang the expense, get whatever you want!"

I can't remember what she was wearing that day. I know what I was wearing: my dungarees and my grungy grey vest. It was too hot for boots, but I'd got these ancient old trainers with the soles flapping. It was like a gesture: this is me, this is who I am, take it or leave it. I didn't dress up for anyone. Anyway, it was boiling hot and our class were acting as stewards, which meant a lot of standing around and being polite. You needed to be comfortable to be polite.

My mum and dad arrived shortly after Emma's. As we watched them moving off across the grass, Emma sighed and said, "Your mum is truly beautiful."

I said, "Mmm," and went on fanning myself with the wodge of programmes I was holding. I was so used to people saying Mum was beautiful, I didn't really hear it anymore.

"It must be so nice to have a mum like that."

"What?" I spun round accusingly. "What's wrong with your mum?"

"Everything," said Emma.

"How can you say that? Your mum's lovely!"

"She's not," said Emma. "She's a mess! She looks like Bramble when he needs a haircut."

Bramble is Emma's dog; he's very big and shaggy. I could sort of see the resemblance. All the same, I thought it was really mean of Emma. Emma's mum is one of my favourite people. She's very warm and jolly and doesn't give a toss what she looks like.

"How can you be so horrid?" I said.

"I'm only telling it like it is," said Emma.

"Your poor mum! When she loves you, and cares about you, and – "

"I'm just saying," said Emma.

"You're just being hateful about her behind her back! Saying she's a mess! I thought you didn't care how people looked?"

"I never said that," said Emma.

I said, "Pardon me?"

"I never said that!"

"Oh? So what did you say?"

"I said it didn't matter if people weren't pretty. I didn't say it didn't matter how they looked. If you just listened, occasionally, instead of ranting on all the time – "

"I don't rant!"

"Of course you do! What d'you think you're

doing now?"

Oh, dear! We got into quite a slanging match. Me and Emma hardly ever fall out, but when we do, we do it big time. The insults fly, no holds barred. We always make up afterwards, as we are such huge friends we really couldn't manage without each other. But while the show is on... beware!

Naturally, you can't expect to hurl insults at the top of your voice without attracting a certain amount of attention, so that before very long we had a crowd of eager onlookers, mainly people from our year, their eyes standing out on stalks and their ears flapping in the breeze. And then, wouldn't you know, a teacher had to come bustling over to see what all the noise was about. Mrs Soames – she's very strict. A real despot. She told Emma to go over to the big marquee and offer her services.

"Do something useful! That's what you're here for."

She then rounded on me and snarled, "Kira Llewellyn, you are a disgrace to the school! How dare you turn up looking like that?"

I was somewhat taken aback, to tell the truth. I mean, what business was it of hers what I looked like? I said, "We were told we could wear what we wanted."

If teachers were still allowed to whack people, I

reckon that's what she would have done. She hissed, "Are you deliberately making a mockery of this occasion? Just go away somewhere and keep out of sight. You're not fit to be on display!"

I really didn't know what right she had to send me away, but I wasn't brave enough to argue. I turned and slunk off, through the middle of the crowd of gawkers. They all fell back to let me pass. I could feel my cheeks begin to burn. It was just so belittling! And then I heard a voice whisper, "Her mother is so gorgeous." And another voice, sneering, in reply: "She knows she can't compete." Laura Brigstock!

I went and hid in the girls' cloakroom. I hated Laura Brigstock, I hated Mrs Soames, I hated Emma, I even hated Mum. Why did I have to go and get lumbered with a mum that made heads turn every time she stepped outside the front door? Emma could have her, and welcome! I'd swop her for Emma's mum any day of the week. Emma's mum was what mums ought to be: warm and cosy and... mumlike. Emma had no idea how I envied her, having a mum like that.

She found me in the cloakroom, a couple of hours later. "Is it true?" she shrieked. "Did Mrs Soames really tell you to go away and keep out of sight?"

Of course they'd all been gossiping; now it would

be round the entire class. I would be a laughing-stock!

"You were pushing it, rather," said Emma. "I mean – " she clapped a hand to her mouth, but not before a vulgar gurgling sound had burst out. "That vest! It looks like someone's mopped the floor with it!"

So amusing. Such a witty turn of phrase. It's nice to have friends; you can always rely on them to back you up. I think not.

By the time I got home, Mum and Dad were already there.

"So what happened to you?" said Dad. "One minute you were there, the next you'd gone."

"Went back indoors," I muttered.

"Hmm! Probably the best place for you." Dad was eyeing my dungarees with considerable distaste. "Not a very good advert for the school dressed like that, are you?"

"Oh, Stuart! Just let her be," said Mum.

"But she makes me ashamed of her," said Dad. "I feel ashamed to own her!"

"Then don't," I snapped. "Pretend I'm a changeling!" With which I rushed out of the room and stormed upstairs, to rage and sulk in private. I knew the minute the door slammed behind me, Mum would start on about how it was just a phase I was going through, and how I would grow out of

it – provided they both kept quiet and didn't nag.
Why did she always have to be so understanding? It
wasn't natural! Even Emma's mum had a go at her
from time to time.

I spent the rest of the afternoon curled up on my
bed having vengeful daydreams in which Mum got
some hideous disfiguring disease that made her not
beautiful any more. That thing teenage boys
sometimes get – well, and girls, too, I suppose. Acne.
All over her face! All pitted and scarred. That would
stop people going on about how beautiful she was.
That would stop Dad drooling, and Jack showing off,
and the grandparents saying how I couldn't hope to
compete.

I know it sounds really mean of me, but it was
only a stupid daydream. I didn't truly want Mum to
be disfigured! And deep down I don't actually believe
that just thinking things can make them happen. I
really don't! Except that people do talk about the
power of prayer, and if praying for good things can
sometimes work –

But I wasn't praying! I was just feeling sorry for
myself and heaping all the blame on Mum. Letting
off steam inside my head. I never wanted anything
bad to happen to her!

Perhaps the bad thing would have happened
anyway. After all, I wasn't the one that caused a pile-

up on the M25; I wasn't the one responsible for Mum being there at just the wrong moment. Pile-ups are always happening, and it had been Mum's decision to go and visit Gran and Grandad in the middle of the week. Nothing to do with me! Gran had shingles, and Grandad couldn't cope. Nobody, but nobody, could have said that it was my fault.

Nobody except me. I knew that it was my fault. If it hadn't been for me, Mum might have left a bit later, a bit earlier, even gone on a different day altogether. But I couldn't say any of this to Dad. How could I ever admit the thoughts that had gone through my head?

"Try to be brave," said Dad. "Mum needs us to be brave!"

So I tried very hard, because everyone else, it seemed, was falling to pieces. Not Dad; Dad was terrific. But Jack, and all the rest of the family. Especially some of the old aunties.

"Oh, not her poor face!" wailed Auntie Trina, racing round to lend support and promptly bursting into tears. "Anything but her face!"

Dad was quite cross. He said to us, after she had gone, that that was downright wicked. "At least your mum's been spared any really serious injury. Nothing life-threatening. Let's just be grateful for that!"

But next day, when Jack and I were allowed to visit, Dad warned us that Mum had been "quite badly knocked about." He said he wanted us to be prepared.

"It's going to be a shock, but the last thing Mum needs is for you to show it. OK?"

We both nodded. "OK!" Then Jack, with an air of bravado, looked across at me and said, "Got that, Dipstick?" Which is one of his stupid names for me.

"Your sister will be all right," said Dad. "Don't you worry about her; you just worry about yourself. But Kira, poppet! Haven't you got something pretty you could put on? That get-up makes you look like a middle-aged woman!"

I'd deliberately chosen the most boring clothes I could find – a denim skirt, dim and dowdy, and a yucky blue blouse to go with it. It seemed to me it would be, like, really tactless to get dressed up when poor Mum was lying there with her face all battered and bruised. Dad, however, insisted that I go and find something else. He said that Mum needed cheering up and would like to see me looking pretty for a change.

Well! I wasn't at all sure that he was right, but I did what he wanted. I put on a pink dress that Mum had bought me ages ago and that I'd always refused to wear on the grounds that it was too girly. Dad was really pleased. He beamed and said, "That's more like it!" Just for a moment, I felt happy that I'd got his approval, but then Jack had to go and ruin it by saying that the pink dress wasn't me.

"You'd look better in a bin bag."

"Just be quiet," said Dad. "Let's focus all our attention on Mum, shall we?"

In spite of Dad doing his best to prepare us, it still came as a shock to see our beautiful Mum lying there with stitches all over her face. I tried really, really hard not to cry, but the tears would come, no matter how furiously I blinked and fought to keep them at bay. Mum laughed, as well as she could, and told me not to be so silly.

"I'm still alive, aren't I? I know I must look a sight, but I hope I do have other things going for me… well, I've got you, for a start, haven't I?" And then she hugged me and said, "I'm so glad you wore that dress! You look so lovely in it."

It wasn't till we left the hospital that Jack finally opened his mouth. He hadn't said a word all the time we'd been with Mum. And then he blurted it out: "Is she always going to look like that?"

Dad did his best to reassure us. "There's a lot they can do! The scars will fade."

But we both knew that Mum would never regain her former beauty.

"What will she do?" whispered Jack. I saw his lip quiver, and I guessed that he was going to find it harder than any of us, even Mum, to come to terms with what had happened.

"What will she do?" Dad looked at Jack reproachfully. "She'll fight, that's what she'll do. She'll fight, and she'll come through. Your mother's not just a pretty face, you know... She's a very special person."

I think that was almost the first time in my life that I really saw Mum as a person in her own right, rather than as just my mum, or the family beauty. I slipped my arm through Dad's.

"She is, isn't she?" I said.

"What's that?" said Dad.

"Mum," I said. "She's a very special person!"

Sing

LINDA NEWBERY

Afterwards, in her room, she could only keep going over and over the way things had been – normal, everyday, ordinary, predictable, safe – and then, in a few moments, not normal.

Her key in the lock. The door swinging open. She slung her coat across the banister, dumped her schoolbag on the floor. "Hi, Mum!" she called, as she always did.

No answering call, but, from the front room, Mum's voice: talking on the phone, rushed and furtive. "Look, I can't talk now. I'll ring you back – later."

And she seemed somehow unnaturally bright and casual as she came to give Jo a welcome-home kiss. "Hello, Jozie! Had a good day?"

Jozie was Mum's special name for Jo, the name no one else ever called her. With Dad it was Jo-Jo. Jo looked at her sharply. "Who was that?"

"Who was what?"

"On the phone!"

"Oh!" Mum gave a nervous little laugh. "Just an old friend. I'll put the kettle on. Or do you want juice?"

"Tea's fine."

In the kitchen. Mum busied herself with filling the kettle and clinking mugs and getting milk out of the fridge, turning her back on Jo.

"What old friend?" Jo persisted, standing in the doorway. "Someone I know?"

"No."

"Well, what's her name?" Jo asked, watching closely.

A hesitation. A definite hesitation. Then: "Chris."

"Who's she? Why've I never heard of her?"

"I know lots of people you've never heard of, Jozie," Mum said, in a voice that was meant to be light and teasing. And she bent to pick up the cat saucer, so that her hair flopped forward and hid her face. Jo knew that technique. It was one she used herself.

Only when she was up in her room, changing out of her uniform, did the thought slam into her brain.

Chris. It had been her own instant assumption that Mum's old friend was a woman. But Chris was a man's name, too. That was why Mum had hesitated, but hadn't put Jo right – nor explained anything at all, come to that.

Mum was keeping a secret – wasn't telling the truth. That could mean only one thing, couldn't it?

An affair.

But – Mum…

Mum wouldn't do anything like that, wouldn't tell lies and keep secrets! Not Mum. Jo was – had been till now – quite confident about that. After all, she thought, tugging on her jeans, there was Dad. Good old Dad. He might be annoying at times, with his irritating habits like making daft jokes that Mum and Jo had heard five thousand times, and never fetching a new loo roll when the old one was used up, but he was Dad, and good to have around. He and Mum were – well, solid. Other people's parents might mess each other about, but Mum and Dad never would. Jo knew that.

Thought she knew that.

And now? But why? Who was this Chris person? Jo only knew that she hated him.

She scowled at her reflection in the mirror, fingered a redness on her chin that looked like it was erupting into a spot, and decided there was only one thing to do. Nothing. Just watch and wait. Keep a careful eye on Mum.

By next morning, Jo was already wondering why she'd been so daft. Everything was exactly the same as usual – the three of them, getting ready for work and school. Dad was burning toast and getting black crumbs in the butter; Mum, who worked mornings at the doctors' surgery, was cleaning shoes by the sink; Jo was reminding her about choir after school; and Flicker the cat was getting under everyone's feet.

Jo might have forgotten all about the Chris question, if it hadn't been for Sophie going to the dentist.

Usually, on gospel-choir days, Jo went round to Sophie's after school, and they had Coke and biscuits in Sophie's bedroom till it was time to go round to the church. Jo had only started going at the start of term, three weeks before, and she wasn't really a proper part of the group since she didn't go to church, but she did love the singing. She didn't believe in God either – or didn't think she did; it was hard to be sure – but the songs were great. *He's got the whole world in his hands… Oh happy day… Lean on me…* However dull or depressed she might feel when she started, the singing – and hearing everyone else sing – raised her spirits so high that she couldn't help skipping along the pavement on the way home, humming to herself. The songs were black songs, Sophie said, and most of the people at the New Testament Church of God were black, like Sophie, but they didn't mind a white person singing their songs, and anyway, Jo tried to explain to Sophie, she *felt* black while she was singing them. She felt just the same as everyone else, carried by the music. When she put all her energy into singing, her voice – though sometimes she couldn't even hear it – was part of the great surging wave of rhythm and sound that filled her ears and her mind and her body. It made her feel alive in a way that nothing else could. There was a lot of laughing, too; it wasn't at all solemn, slow or dreary, the way hymn-singing could sometimes be. This was a special kind of hymn, joyous and energetic. Noleen, the choir leader, was so animated that her whole body – her sweeping arm, her swinging hair, her swaying hips – seemed to be making the music. When there was a very sad song, she'd seem completely weighed down by it, still and silent as the last chord faded away, and then she'd break into a big, brilliant smile and they'd all know they'd done well. Together. They were a team.

So this time Sophie went off to the dentist, and Jo headed home, and they agreed to meet at the church an hour later.

And although Jo had mentioned this arrangement at breakfast, Mum had forgotten.

As Jo let herself in, Mum was letting herself out. The first thing Jo noticed was how startled she looked. And the second thing, how dressed-up she was for a Tuesday afternoon. She was wearing her new grey jacket, and the silky mauve scarf that Jo liked, and silver stud earrings, and make-up. Even lipstick. Mum only ever wore lipstick for occasions like Parents' Evenings at school. Never for work. Never to go out in the daytime. Never to go out with Dad.

"Oh – Jo!" Mum breezed, or at least tried to breeze.

And the walls came tumbling down. That was a line from one of the songs. Jo felt her walls were tumbling down, all around her. The walls that were home, and family, and everything that was safe and normal. Yesterday had shown her the first creeping crack; she had felt the first tremor, and tried to ignore it. But how could you ignore an earthquake?

"Where are you off to?" Jo demanded.

"I'm meeting someone," Mum said, not quite meeting her eye.

"Chris, I suppose?"

The front path was narrow, and Jo was blocking it. Mum tried to sidestep.

"Chris?" Mum repeated, as if making sure she'd heard right. Then: "Yes, actually."

Guilt! Guilt, written all over her!

"Does Dad know?" Jo said, not giving way.

"Excuse me, love, I don't want to be late. Yes, of course he does." Mum sidestepped; Jo inhaled a whiff of perfume. "Look, Jo – I'll – I'll tell you all about it later," she threw over her shoulder. "I'm sorry."

Dad knows! So it's not even a secret!

That makes it even worse, doesn't it?

And Mum's sorry – but not sorry enough to stop doing it…

Jo went inside, closed the door, dumped her bag; then sneaked out again, to the front gate. She looked along the street in the direction Mum had gone.

There was Mum, walking quickly, one tail of her mauve scarf fluttering out jauntily behind her, clop-clopping in her smart shoes – her smart shoes, the ones that made her feet hurt if she walked far in them – to the corner. There, not turning right for the bus-stop, but getting into a silver Focus that was waiting there. After a few moments, it drove off. Jo couldn't see who was driving, but obviously it was Him. It was Chris. It was Chris she'd got all dressed up for, with lipstick and perfume and smart shoes. And that pause! Long enough for – what? A kiss? Gazing into each other's eyes? For Mum to say, "I've made up my mind. I'm leaving them. I've got to be with you, Chris."

I hate him! I hate him!

And she couldn't be quite sure that she didn't hate Mum, too.

As she went back indoors and up to her room, Jo

was aching inside in a way she hadn't ached since her guinea-pig died. She flung herself on her bed and lay staring at the ceiling. She didn't feel like going to choir now – didn't feel like doing anything at all, but she couldn't stay here at home. Home? How much longer would it be home? Tonight, Mum was going to tell them. Chris was going to steal her away. No, it wouldn't even be stealing – it was Mum's own choice.

Jo hadn't caught even a glimpse of Chris, not even a shadowy presence in the car, but she'd formed a picture of him in her mind. He was tall, with a bony face. Fairish hair that was thinning a bit. He'd be not exactly good-looking, but still the sort of man women could be silly about, like Mr Ballard, her science teacher. He'd be full of compliments and flattery and smarmy smiles. He'd wear bright jokey ties, and shoes with buckles.

And he'd have had other girlfriends before Mum. Other married girlfriends.

How could Mum fall for someone like that; how could she? Jo didn't know whether she wanted to scream, or cry, or go into her parents' bedroom and smash Mum's favourite crystal vase to bits.

So she sang. She went to choir and pretended to everyone, even to Sophie, that nothing was wrong, and she tried to let all her anger and anxiety pour out with the notes, and tried to let the singing warm her whole body, the way it could. Today, though, she could only remember how happy she usually was at choir practice; already it seemed weeks ago that she hadn't been weighted with worry and doubt. Anyway, how long had it been going on, the Mum-and-Chris thing? And did that mean she'd been wrongly, innocently, ignorantly happy, unsuspecting?

Next, to make things even worse, she came close to quarrelling with Sophie. Only close, because Sophie didn't really do quarrelling; but still, after Sophie had tried three times to find out what was wrong, and Jo had tossed her head and said, "Nothing," and "I said, nothing," and finally, "Look, give it a rest, will you?" Sophie said, "OK! See you tomorrow – if you're speaking to me, that is," and went off home in what was very nearly a huff.

Jo hurried home, even though part of her wanted to drag her feet and put off hearing what Mum had to say.

🦋 🦋 🦋

"I owe you an explanation, Jo," Mum said.

Here they were, in the kitchen, all three of them, and even Flicker purring on Dad's lap, making four. Dad had made hot chocolate, and it was going to be Confession Time. Only Mum didn't look the smallest bit guilty – excited, rather. She'd changed out of her smart clothes into jeans and trainers, but she still had make-up and earrings on. Dad wasn't playing the part of Deceived Husband, either. Mum was standing by the sink, and Dad was looking at her in a comfortable, affectionate – even, Jo thought, *adoring* – sort of way.

Now what's going on? Mum's changed her mind? Come to her senses? Told Chris where to get off?

"It's about that Chris, isn't it?" Jo said, prickly and defensive. "I know you've been seeing him."

Mum looked startled. "Him? No! Whatever made you think that? Oh, Jozie, I'm sorry – is that what you've been thinking?" She came over and gave Jo a big, perfume-scented hug. "Chris is – Jo, Chris is my mother."

"Mother?"

Jo tried to get hold of the word. It seemed to have shrugged off its usual meaning, and wriggled itself into a new and different one. She felt dizzy – the kitchen walls and cupboards were swimming in front of her, the table no longer firmly standing on the floor.

"But," she said, "Gran's your mother."

She knew this wasn't true, of course. She'd known for years, since she was about six, that Mum was adopted. But somehow that fact had got filed away in the back of her mind, and had become just one of the countless things she kept in there; she never took it out to look at it. That was because of Gran and Grandad, really. She didn't want to deny them their proper place in the family. Of course, they weren't really her grandparents, but that wasn't something she ever thought about, or wanted to.

Mum looked at her. "Gran and Grandad are my mum and dad. They adopted me. They chose me. They looked after me and they love me and they love you, Jo, very much. But Mum's not my birth-mother and Grandad isn't my real father. You know that."

"Yes," Jo conceded. But knowing wasn't the same as taking in. She had never wanted to believe that, if Gran wasn't Mum's mum, someone else must be. Knowing how silly it would sound to come out with this, she was silent.

"Chris is my birth-mother," Mum said, looking at Jo closely, as if to make quite sure she understood.

"But you told me you didn't know her!" Jo burst out. "Didn't want to. She gave you up for adoption, didn't she?"

Mum looked down at the mug she was holding. "For a long time I didn't know her. But then I got curious. Curiouser and curiouser, till I couldn't stop thinking about it. So I found out about Chris, and got in touch, and first met her three years ago."

"Three years ago?" Jo shouted. "And you never said?"

Mum and Dad exchanged glances.

"Perhaps I should have told you," Mum said, with a rueful little smile. "I thought you were too young. I was waiting to tell you when the time was right."

"What, you mean you've been meeting this Chris person, and talking on the phone for three years, and I haven't known?"

"No," said Mum. "She lives a long way away, in Nottingham. She's married, with two grown-up children. We haven't been seeing each other. We sometimes write, and I've sent her photos of you."

"So why now? Why's she in London, not Nottingham?"

Mum looked at Dad, and this time it was Dad who answered. "Mum wanted to know who her father is."

"Father?" Jo repeated. Not only had this stranger turned up (this complete stranger who had photos of Jo!), but there was another unknown person out there too – Mum's father. Jo's real grandfather. Of course, there had to be.

"She wouldn't tell me, the first time we met," Mum explained. "But this time, she did."

"Why?"

"Because of you, Jozie."

"Because of me? What have I got to do with it?"

"Quite a lot," said Mum.

"Go on, then," Dad prompted.

Mum shifted on her stool, settling herself. "Well, this is how Chris told it. She lived in Walthamstow when she was a teenager – "

"Where's that?"

"Other side of London, out towards Essex. She didn't get on well with her parents, and often spent nights at her best friend's house. She didn't like school much – that was one of the things they argued about, and she left when she was sixteen. Worked at waitressing, worked in shops – whatever she could find. She never wanted to settle at one thing. She liked the feeling that she could up and leave whenever she felt like it, and move on to something new."

Jo leaned forward, listening hard, wanting to remember every word.

"She was seventeen when she met him. She had a job in a souvenir shop at Piccadilly Circus. She liked that, she said. Liked meeting loads of people, all the tourists who came into the shop, liked being in Piccadilly where there was lots going on. To get to work, she used to get on at Walthamstow, get the Central Line to Oxford Circus, and change for Piccadilly. That meant going through the tunnels along with all the people going to work, all the business people with their suits and briefcases and newspapers."

Jo waited for one of these people to step forward and enter the story. Was Mum's father – her grandfather – one of the tourists in the souvenir shop? One of the businessmen in a smart suit? Who did she want him to be?

"It was his voice she heard first. One morning she was in the tunnel, going from the Central Line to the Bakerloo, when she heard this voice, this wonderful clear voice, carrying above everyone's heads and their footsteps in the subway. He was playing a guitar and singing. She was used to seeing buskers, but this time she was keen to see who the voice belonged to. And there he was. Everyone else in the tunnel was sort of grey and drab, she said, all hurrying to get to their banks and offices and shops, all in their smart clothes, no one talking or laughing or even looking at each other, as if they were all robots. And then there he was. Playing his guitar, filling the tunnel with its sound, and his singing. He was singing 'Yesterday' – you know? – and it's funny, I've always liked that. Nearly everyone was hurrying past him without even a glance, but Chris slowed down and looked, even though she was already late for work. It was as if he was singing just for her. She fell in love with his voice, then with his face. He was looking up at the roof of the tunnel, over everyone's head. He looked sort of lit up, she said. He was so intent on his singing, pouring his whole self into it, that he didn't even care if no one was taking the slightest notice."

"Did she give him some money? Stop and talk to him?"

"She slowed down. She walked past him, looking, then looking back. Just for a moment their eyes met, and it felt like a sort of promise. She reached her own platform and waited for her train. When it came, she got on as usual. It was always crowded, so she didn't get a seat, she had to stand there jammed in with the other strap-hangers. Then, just as the doors were closing, she pushed through the other passengers and jumped off. She had to go back."

"What did she do?"

"It was hard, pushing through the flow of people all coming the other way, but she did it. Whenever she thinks of it, she says, and she knows this makes no sense at all, she sees him lit up by a shaft of sunlight, golden in the middle of all that drabness. She stopped and stood in front of him. He saw her, but carried on with his song – a different one now – right to the end. Then she said, 'I've come back.'"

"Just like that?"

Mum nodded. "Just like that."

"And what did he say?"

"Nothing at first. He didn't seem surprised. It was as if he'd expected her to come back to him. He sang one more song, looking at her, and she felt the thrill of it through her whole body. Then he picked up the coins from his guitar case – not many – and put them in his pocket. He put his guitar away. And they walked together along the tunnel and away from the trains and up the steps, and out into the sunshine."

"What about her job? Was she late?"

"She'd forgotten all about it. She was with him now. They walked along to Hyde Park, and they walked and they talked and they spent all day together. And sometimes he sang and he played just for her."

"What was his name?"

"She never found out. By the time she thought of asking, he'd gone."

"Gone? What happened after they'd spent all day in the park?"

"They spent all night in the park too. It was the beginning of summer. She knows he was with her when it first got light, but then she slept some more and when she woke up he was gone. He'd left her a little bunch of daisies, on the grass beside her, carefully tied with a stem of grass, and that was all."

"Was she sad? Angry?"

Mum shook her head. "Most of all, she felt happy. As if he'd passed on some of his lit-up-ness to her. She felt warm and glowing inside. She kept humming 'Yesterday' – because, now, it was yesterday she wanted. She tried to find him, she went back to Oxford Circus and searched the tunnels, but there was only one busker and it wasn't him. She searched and she searched, all the other stations, the underpasses, wherever there were buskers. But she knew, she just knew, she'd never see him again. He'd passed through her life and moved on somewhere else. She almost began to wonder if he'd been real, or if she'd just imagined him. She began to think it was like a sort of spell – he had to stay underground, and he could leave and come up to the sunlight when somebody stopped and spoke to him, but only for one day. Then he'd have to go back underground, somewhere she couldn't find him. He left her something real enough, though. He left her – well, me."

"She was pregnant?"

"She found out a little while later. Her parents were furious, especially as she didn't know his name, knew nothing that could find him. They said horrible things, told her she was cheap and a disgrace to the family. It was because of them she gave me up for adoption. She didn't want to, but finally she gave in. She always, always regretted it, she said."

Dad was shaking his head. "This whole story – the way she told you – sounds a bit fanciful, to me. She was in trouble, and wanted to make it sound like something from a fairy-tale, or a Greek myth, instead of – well – a one-night stand with a complete stranger."

"Dad!" Jo reproached. She thought it was wonderful. Her grandfather was someone who would never grow old, who could enchant with his voice, who could hand on his radiance like a golden torch.

"What did you mean," she asked her mother, "when you said Chris told you because of me?"

"I told her how you love to sing," Mum said. "She always thought I might be a singer – she might find me singing in concerts or operas or something. Me, who can't even sing in tune! No, it's skipped a generation, Jozie. He's passed it straight on to you. It's his gift."

In bed, Jo thought about what it would be like to be Mum. She'd been wrong, unfair and wrong, to suspect Mum. Now she wondered what it was like, growing up without knowing who her mother and father were – with big blanks in her life. That must mean she didn't really know who she was. But she hadn't let it stop her from making a family of her own that was safe and strong. Now she was beginning to find out – getting to know her own mother, and hearing the story of the father she would never know. And, however intriguing they were, not letting them replace Gran and Grandad.

Jo thought about singing, too.

She thought about how it made her feel, to open her mouth and sing. It was like nothing else she knew. She was doing it for herself, but taking part in something bigger. The music had its own power and strength, its own waves and rhythm and feelings, its swell and its ebb. It could bring a big choking sob to her throat and tears to her eyes, or it could make her giddy enough to fly. It made her feel she could do anything. It was like nothing else she knew.

❦ ❦ ❦

"Let's go and look for him!" Sophie said, greatly excited.

"He won't be there! This was years and years ago!"

Even if he was, he'd be old now – a man of fifty-something, which Mum said was Chris's age. Jo didn't want him to be fifty. She wanted him to stay youthful and golden, with a strong young voice.

But they had a day off school for a teacher-training day, and they were going shopping in Oxford Street, and they always got off the train at Oxford Circus. It would be silly not to look, even if it was only at the place where he'd stood, and at the tunnel that had been filled by his voice.

"So," said Sophie, marching purposefully up the

steps from the Central Line, "when are you going to meet Chris?"

"Soon. She's going to come round and spend a day with us." Jo felt a little tremor of excitement when she thought about this. What would she say to Chris? What would Chris say to her? Would Chris want to be called Gran? Because that was what she was, even though she didn't sound like a grandmother. Jo could only think of her as the girl who had fallen in love with a voice. "Then there are Chris's children!" she told Sophie. "Grown-up, in their twenties. Mum hasn't met them yet, but they're her half-brother and sister."

"And your half-aunt and half-uncle," said Sophie. "You lucky thing! But they're not related to him, are they? Not like you."

Jo thought of the line from her grandfather as a thread spun of fine gold, almost invisible, so fragile that it would easily snap, connecting him to Mum, and Mum to Jo. She must hold it and never let go. She held another line too, tougher and stronger and more like a rope, from Gran and Grandad to Mum and herself. Now she had both.

It wasn't the rush-hour, and the connecting tunnel wasn't full of marching feet. Only a few odd people were coming through – three teenage boys, an old man, two women with carrier bags – and there was no busker at all, though the official pitch was marked. Jo felt disappointed, even though disappointment was what she'd expected.

Sophie didn't give up so easily. "Come on! We'll go round the whole station."

Up and down escalators they went, along platforms and walkways, round corners, up steps, down steps – Central Line, Bakerloo, Victoria, Bakerloo, Central. Only one busker in the whole station – a girl with a flute, just packing up. She didn't look like someone bewitched by a spell, fated to stay underground till the spell was broken. She had a can of Coke and a copy of *Time Out* and very trendy trainers.

"Hi," Jo said, just in case.

"We might as well go to Topshop," Sophie said. "We can look again later."

"OK." Jo tried to push away the feeling that the whole thing was pointless.

They were walking along the tunnel towards a sign saying WAY OUT. Sophie stopped, tilting her head.

"Listen!"

Jo turned the same way. Yes – music, voices, not one but several, pure and happy, coming from somewhere down below...

Sophie tugged at her arm. "This way!"

They ran towards the sound, bumping against each other in their hurry, skittering round a corner and down a stairway. And there they were, the singers, at the bottom of steps that separated two platforms. Their voices rose and fell sweetly in harmony – a boy and three girls, a few years older than Jo. No guitar, no accompaniment, no hat or instrument on the ground for coins: they were just singing for themselves. The song was "Tomorrow", one that Jo knew from the school production last year. It was sad and yearning, sung as a solo, but now – with the voices mingling and sharing, one singing a snatch then passing it on to another – Jo heard only happiness, the notes bubbling with laughter. They held on to the last chord, singing their different notes, pure and echoey, the sound filling the stairwell. It seemed to hang in the air before fading slowly to silence. After a pause, they burst out laughing, delighted with themselves. One of the girls looked around at Sophie and Jo, a bit embarrassed, but her eyes were shining, her face flushed with singing.

Then the whoosh and rush of a train in the tunnel, a gust of hot air, and the blur of windows and doors gradually becoming clear as it halted. One of the girls, the one who had looked around, was getting on the train; the others hugged her and waved. She saw Jo watching, and waved at her too as the doors slid together; then she stood looking through the window until the train carried her into darkness. Her friends, chatting, moved through to the platform on the other side.

"They were nice," Jo said. "I wonder where she's going? And how they know each other? And when they'll see each other again?"

"I felt like joining in," said Sophie. "And I bet they wouldn't have minded."

That's what it must have been like, Jo thought, *the voice filling the tunnel with life and promise.* She thought of Chris standing inside the train, and that second when she'd jumped off again: that split-second decision that had brought Mum into being, and therefore Jo. *I wouldn't exist if she'd stayed on the train and gone to work as usual,* Jo thought, and that gave her a funny, swimmy feeling inside.

Sophie was humming "Tomorrow" as she led the way back towards the exit.

But she was here; it had happened this way and not that, and she had her gift, her golden gift handed across two generations. It was hers, to keep. She could sing.

Pausing, she looked back at the place where the group of friends had stood, lighting up the day. Then she bounded after Sophie, two steps at a time, snatching a phrase of the song and running ahead. She was full of singing, alive with it, almost bursting.

Missing Out

BETTY HICKS

Jack, my nine-year-old stepbrother, ate a mealworm. Is that gross, or what?

When Dad married Alice, I inherited not one crazy brother, but three, along with a super-messy house. Ever since then, I stay busy deciding: is the stuff they do disgusting, or cool?

When I visit Mom's house, there are no decisions. At precisely seven o'clock, the two of us sit down to dinner in her deluxe townhouse. Oriental rugs, a complete leather-bound collection of Shakespeare with raised gold lettering that I love to run my fingers across, incredible orchid collection, fine china, *filet mignon* with a reduced Burgundy sauce, and asparagus with toasted almonds.

Mom is a great cook.

She's also beautiful. More than beautiful, she's elegant. You'd never guess we were related. Her long brown hair shines like the mahogany dining-room table that my elbows are propped on. She wears it pulled back in one long, perfect plait, every hair in place.

My hair is boring brown, like a mouse, and insanely curly. I pull it back in a ponytail, but most of the pieces escape the rubber band and frizz around my face. A plait is out of the question.

"Elizabeth," says Mom, gracefully draping a perfectly pressed linen napkin across her lap. "How are things at your dad's house?"

"Great!" I blurt, then immediately regret it. Mom's face has pinched up as if she swallowed a fish bone.

But life at Dad's house *is* great – three stepbrothers who make me laugh, and a stepmother who doesn't freak if my bed's not made.

Mom reclaims her normal face, but her voice is definitely tense. "And the dot-com business?" she asks.

Dad's a commercial artist. He started an internet business selling customised T-shirt designs, but it failed. Mom knows that, because I told her a month ago, just after she flew back from Paris. She said Dad should've had his marketing money in sync with I-forget-what. Some business word.

All I want to know is, where is the mom who used to laugh at my knock-knock jokes and read me fairy tales? The one who acted out the wicked-witch parts while I giggled? When did she turn so super serious? And so boring?

I defend him. "He's got a ton of art jobs right now. Really busy."

Mom carefully cuts one asparagus spear into four perfect bites. "Elizabeth," she says. "I've missed you."

"Me too, Mom." I mean it. I have missed her. Especially the mom I remember, the one who didn't jet all over the world making tons of money as an international business consultant. That's why I live with Dad. Because she's never home.

But I miss Dad's house even more – the noise, my messy room, the dirty dishes that no one's ever in a hurry to wash. It's the new me.

"Uh, Mom." I don't know how to bring this up, but I love my new name, too.

Just say it, I tell myself.

"Mom. Did you know my friends call me 'Iz' now?" Actually, it's my new brothers who call me Iz, but I think, *Don't go there. Not now.*

"What?" she asks.

"Iz," I repeat.

"Oh," she chuckles. "Kids come up with the craziest things."

"No, Mom. It's my name now. Honest."

"Is?" she asks, in a foggy voice.

"Yeah, Iz," I say for the third time.

Mom wrinkles her forehead and tilts her head oddly. "Is is not a name," she says. "It's a verb."

"Huh?"

"A verb," she repeats. "Is is a verb."

"Oh." I get it. "It's not I-s. It's I-z. You know, Liz without the L. Iz."

"Iz?" Her eyes open wide. "But, sweetheart, you have a beautiful name. Elizabeth Ellington Becker. You want me to call you Iz?"

"Yep," I say, hoping I sound confident. "Iz Becker. That's me." I smile.

Mom circles her fork around and around in her reduction sauce, making little rivers of it all over her Herend china plate.

"OK," she says finally. "If you're sure."

"I'm sure."

For a long time, neither of us says a word.

She sighs a couple of times and gazes off into space. Probably picturing Elizabeth Ellington Becker, the beautiful, promising newborn baby who, eleven years later, turned into a verb.

Finally, she stands up to clear the dishes and, out of nowhere, says, "How would you like a pet that stayed at my house?"

"A dog!" I screech. I can't believe it. "I'm getting a dog?"

I've wanted a dog forever. Dad and Alice claim our house has enough chaos already, and Mom's place has no room for dog hairs.

"No," she says gently. "Not a dog. Go and look in your room."

I fly up the stairs. There, on top of my bookcase, is an aquarium, complete with pumps and fancy filters. Swimming around in it are five of the most amazing tropical fish I've ever seen. Bright blues, greens, and yellows. They make all the goldfish at Dad's house look like sick guppies.

Mom is going to keep an aquarium? Does she know what a dirty fish tank smells like when you clean it? Gag. Would Mom do that? For me?

"What do you think?" she says, slipping into the room behind me.

I turn and hug her. "They're beautiful," I say. "But, who's going to clean the tank?" OK, that's not the second thing that should have come out of my mouth, but it did.

Well," she answers, slipping an arm around my shoulders, "we could do it together."

"But you're never here."

She gives me an extra squeeze. "Maybe I can stay at home more."

"But who's going to feed them when you're not here?" My brain is still trying to understand what Mom-buying-complicated-fish means.

"The lady who comes to water my orchids," she answers.

"Oh." I stare at my fish. They're gorgeous. So why am I not more thrilled? The fish are graceful and elegant. Like my mother. And isn't she more like my old mom? The one that I miss? I should be happy.

By the next day, I am happy. Mom jets back to England, and I'm at home with Dad and the new, bigger, Becker family. Two days later, Mom calls from London.

"Sweetheart," she says. The phone connection is so clear, I feel as if she's in the next room. Her voice sounds more relaxed than I've heard in forever. "How's my sunshine?"

"Great, Mom. What's up?"

"I'll be home again next Thursday," she says.

"Cool." A part of me really does think it's cool, but another part of me doesn't want to stay with her again so soon. If I leave my house, even for a night, I always miss something awesome. Last time, Jack and Joey and Logan dug a hole in the back garden big enough to put a cow in.

I hate missing out.

"And Eliz – I mean, Iz, I have wonderful news."

"Yeah?" I ask. Maybe she's moving to France to be closer to her work. Would that be good news – or bad?

"I miss you," she says, suddenly sounding more serious. "I'm going to stop travelling and work in

town. I'll do small consulting jobs. Less money, but" –
I could hear the excitement building in her voice –
"life's not about money, is it?"

"Uh, no, Mom. Of course not." She's going to live
here. Permanently. What does that mean?

"Don't you see what that means, Elizabeth? It
means you can live with me now."

A million thoughts whiz through my brain like
bullets. Live with Mom? No more Dad and Alice?
No more wacky pizza nights, video-game
marathons? No more brothers to jump into leaf piles
with? Nobody who eats mealworms?

I don't answer.

She knows I don't answer.

We leave it hanging.

For the rest of the week, I can't think about it.
Then on Friday, after school, I go to Mom's, with
enough clothes to stay three nights. No more.

All day, I practise telling her that I don't want to
live there. I am so ready.

Who am I kidding? I'll never be ready to tell her
that.

I plop down in my seat for dinner, and can't
believe my eyes. I'm staring at a hamburger, French
fries, and purple ketchup!

Mom's beautifully polished table is set with
expensive china, Brussels-lace placemats, and antique

silver. In the centre sits a plastic squeeze bottle full of purple goop, as out of place as a mangy mutt at a dog show.

"Purple ketchup?" I ask, dismayed. How has Mom made the move from Burgundy reduction sauce to purple ketchup?

"Do you like it?" she asks. "It's the latest thing in kids' products."

I pick it up and squeeze purple sauce onto my fine china plate. It clashes totally with the delicate, hand-painted, coral-colored birds. This is crazy. So not Mom. Here she is doing stupid stuff, buying tropical fish and insanely dyed ketchup, and for what? For me?

I don't know whether to laugh or cry, but I've definitely lost my appetite.

"Well," says Mom, clearly disappointed, "don't eat it if you don't want to."

Reluctantly, I pick up a French fry, dip it in the purple puddle on my plate, and pop it into my mouth. My brain expects a taste like grape juice, but it's plain old tomato ketchup. I chew slowly, force myself to swallow, and smile.

"Yum," I lie. Not that it tastes bad. Any other day, it would've been delicious – and fun. But right now the tube connecting my mouth to my stomach is so clogged with guilt that food won't fit.

Tell her the truth. You don't want to live with her!

"I rented a movie for us to watch," she says. I hear the hope in her voice.

"Great," I say, thinking, *I have three whole days. Why not wait?*

The movie is fun, and the next day, Saturday, starts out nice, but so peaceful it numbs my mind. I try not to think what I'm missing at home.

Meanwhile, Mom is killing herself to make me happy. She wants to redo my room. I can pick anything I want. Striped curtains or flowered ones? Do I need new software? Games? Clothes? Let's go shopping.

I have to tell her. Now. Guilt is covering me like a giant cobweb, clinging, smothering.

"Mom."

"Let's play tennis," she says.

Tennis? Do I play tennis? Does Mom play tennis?

"I signed us up for lessons," she explains with a perky smile.

"Mom. No. Some other time. OK? We need to talk."

"How about ice cream," she answers. "You still love ice cream. Right?"

The next thing I know we're at Baskin Robbins.

I order a sugar cone of something called Triple Fudge Mudslide. Mom gets a cup of pistachio. We sit outdoors at a tiny pink wrought-iron table that's supposed to make customers think they're eating ice cream back in the fifties – before stepfamilies were invented.

I lick my super-rich creamy chocolate and think about what to say.

"Mom," I give it my best shot. "This is fun."

She beams. "We can do this everyday."

"Mom," I start again, "I love you."

She stops her spoon midway to her mouth, and lowers it slowly back into her ice-cream cup. "I love you, too," she says, cautiously.

We both know I said "I love you", but the way I said it meant, "I love you, but…"

She waits.

"Mom." I begin again, slowly, just like I practised. "You know I wanted to live with you when Dad got married." I swallow and take a deep breath. "But since then I've got used to my new family. More than used to them, Mom. I love them. We have fun."

All that comes out faster than I mean it to, but I said it! I feel weird – all bubbly and flat at the same time. I stare at my ice-cream cone so I won't have to see what Mom's face is doing.

"I love you," I repeat. "I loved our day together. I love my new fish. I want to be with you. Honest. But, just sometimes. Not all the time."

For about a century, nobody says a word. My ice

cream starts to drip down my hand, so I lick it. But still, I don't look up.

More silence. When Mom finally speaks, her voice is strange – almost casual, as if we've been talking about the weather.

"I've thought about getting a dog," she says. "Would you like a dog?"

Late that night, I lie awake in my bed at Mom's house, listening to the hum of pumps and filters on my fancy new aquarium, and ask myself, *Do I love my mother, or do I hate my mother?*

I finally get up the nerve to tell her that I want to live with Dad, and what does she do? She bribes me! With a dog! And acts as if I never said a word!

My first reaction was surprise, followed by disgust, then anger. How could she be that shameless? Does she think I'm stupid?

My second reaction, the one that I will never, ever tell another living soul, was *What kind of dog?* I hate myself for even thinking it. But I had thought it. I roll over and add it to my growing lump of guilt.

The next morning, I can barely look Mom in the face. She, on the other hand, acts as if I hadn't flung my Triple Fudge Mudslide onto the ground the day before and stomped off to the car. But we both knew I had.

"Blueberry pancakes?" she asks in a perfectly

normal voice, calmly pouring milk into a bowl with flour and eggs.

"No, thanks." I reach for a box of dry cereal.

"How about a bichon frise?" she asks, as though it were a side order to go with the pancakes.

"A what?"

"A bichon. You know – one of those adorable little white dogs that looks kind of like a poodle."

"Mom!" I scream, slamming the cereal box down so hard that Cheerios fly up in the air and spill onto the counter. "Stop! Would you please just stop!? What's the matter with you?!"

Mom quits stirring the batter for the pancakes that I don't want, and gapes at me.

"I don't want a dog!" I scream some more. "I want a family! A big family! Mom. Please. Try to understand."

Tears well up in her large hazel eyes.

"I mean, I do want a dog," I keep going. "You know I want a dog. More than almost anything. But not more than Dad and Alice and Logan and Jack and Joey. Not more than that, Mom."

The tears spill over onto her perfect cheekbones. Her face doesn't contort. Her mascara doesn't run. My mom looks elegant, even when she cries.

I want to hug her. But I still don't want to live with her.

The rest of the day we pretend that nothing happened, but the tension is so heavy I could stuff it into rubbish bags and lug it to the tip.

We eat a quiet dinner, watch a Hallmark made-for-TV movie, and go to bed early. I lie awake asking myself, *Am I a good kid for being honest, or a rotten kid for hurting Mom?*

All I can think about is this weird Australian spider I learned about in science. The female was a great mother. She built a nest for her babies and worked like crazy, catching them insects to eat. And what did the little baby spiders do when they got big enough? They ate her!

No kidding. They started by nibbling her legs off... slowly. I guess she must have hobbled around on stumps for a while, but eventually the kids munched every leg until there weren't any left. When she couldn't move, they chowed down on the rest of her.

I toss and turn forever. Finally, I fall asleep, but I wake myself back up making a strangled grunting noise – the kind you make when you try to scream in your sleep, but your voice won't work.

I sit up straight, sweating and panicked. I've been dreaming that I'm roasting one of Mom's legs on a spit and basting it with purple ketchup.

The next morning, Mom drops me off at school.

"Tennis this afternoon?" she asks hopefully.

"Sure," I grin back, ecstatic that her legs aren't burnt, or nibbled on, or anything. But I know I'm lying. This afternoon, I'm going home. To Dad's house. Like a coward, I leave the message on her answering machine.

She doesn't call back. For a week, I hear nothing. Has she gone back to London?

On Friday, finally, she calls. I expect an icy voice. A hurt voice. But Mom is excited. "Iz! You won't believe this!"

Wow. She sounds the way she used to, before her job sent her all over the planet. What excited her then – besides her wicked–witch imitations? I know. She used to throw fancy dinner parties for Dad and their friends. She loved doing that. Planning elegant menus of stuff that took all day to cook. Creating amazing arrangements of exotic flowers. Picking the perfect CD for background music. All those things used to make Mom this excited.

Was she planning an elegant party for all her friends? Did she still have friends, or had she been away too much? I didn't even know.

Whatever, she wants me to come over. She has a surprise.

"OK," I say, but I'm worried. This can't be good.

When I get to her townhouse, she flings open her door and scurries to the kitchen.

"Wait here," she calls back to me. "Close your eyes."

I don't like the feel of this.

"Are your eyes closed?" asks Mom, peeking her head around the kitchen door and grinning.

"Yes, Mom." I squeeze my eyes shut.

"OK, sweetheart. Open them."

I open my eyes. It takes me half a second to focus. *Oh, my God! What is that?! It can't be!* But it is.

Mom stands proudly by the kitchen door, holding it open. By her feet sits the ugliest dog I've ever seen. Part of me is furious. She's still trying to bribe me with a dog! Another part of me wants to laugh hysterically at the creature sitting by her feet. How could anyone be bribed with *that* dog?

She looks kind of like a bulldog. Same short, bent legs and smushed face. But she's a stick-figure bulldog – something a kid would draw. Skinny. Not starved. Just built thin.

Her eyes lock on to mine and clearly say, *Love me.* I don't know whether to laugh or hug her.

Instead, I yell at Mom.

"Mom!" I shout. "How could you?"

"How could I what?" says Mom, suddenly baffled.

"Keep trying to win me over with stupid stuff!"

Mom's face goes through about a million frames

per second. Surprise, confusion, recognition, horror.

"Oh, Iz!" she exclaims. "No. This dog isn't for you. This dog is for me." She pauses and thinks for a second. "OK, maybe I did try to bribe you before. But not this time." She gazes lovingly at Mystery Mutt, scoops her up, and kisses her, smack on her caved-in nose.

"And this little sunshine is not stupid!" she adds defensively.

I thought I was her sunshine.

Mom puts the dog back on the floor, walks quickly towards me, and folds me into a warm hug. Then she holds me back at arm's length, and says, "Iz, let's sit down."

We walk into the living room. Mom sits on one side of the sofa. I sit on the other. Ugly mutt sits on the floor between us and looks eagerly back and forth.

Mom makes her hands into a steeple in front of her face. She thinks a moment, then lowers them.

"I love you," she says, looking directly into my eyes. "But I understand why you can't move in with me." She hesitates. "I've known it for months."

"Oh, Mom," I interrupt. "Don't – "

"Iz," says Mom, softly. "Shhh. It's all right. Every time I talk to you. From Paris. From London. You've told me. Not in so many words, but in your joy. You have a family that loves you, and you love them, and…" Her voice is suddenly quivery, so she stops.

"It's OK," she says, quietly. Then she laughs. A real, from-the-heart, genuine laugh. "I'd go bonkers in less than two minutes if I lived with that crew. But, it is you." She corrects herself. "It is Iz."

"Oh, Mom." I want to cry. Instead, I reach down and pick up ugly-dog, because she's leaning against my leg, saying, *Excuse me, I'm here.*

"Uh, Mom," I say, stroking one soft, saggy ear. "This is not a bichon."

"No kidding," says Mom, brightening. "That's the other thing I wanted to tell you. Ever since I got your message, I can't tell you how alone I felt."

"Mom," I moan.

"No." She puts out her arm to hold me off. "Let me finish. I went straight to the farmers' market. You know nothing cheers me up like fresh ingredients. I planned to pick out the best lettuces, the most exotic vegetables, and take them home and create a salad that would make the cover of *Gourmet* magazine."

She pauses, puckers her lips, and gently dispatches an air kiss, not at me, but at the dog whose ear I'm scratching.

"They were hosting an Adopt-A-Pet event outside the market," she continues. "Dozens of people were there with pets that needed homes. I walked right by them, of course. What a yapping, whining mixture of mutts. And then I saw her." She gazes tenderly at –

"Mom," I ask, "what is her name?"

"Cleopatra."

"Cleopatra!" I practically choke.

Mom laughs. "I know she's not beautiful, but there is something irresistible about her. The eyes, I think. Besides, you know I love Shakespeare – and *Antony and Cleopatra* is my favourite play. I knew I wanted her before I heard what her name was, but that clinched it."

Mom wiggles her eyebrows up and down, and does a silly, spooky-music imitation that reminds me of her wicked-witch routine. "I think Cleopatra and I are destined to be together," she says. Then she claps her hands together. "The best part is that she's fully grown, so she's already housetrained, and she won't chew on my carpets."

I cup Cleopatra's smashed-in face in my hands. She is so ugly, she's almost cute. "But. Mom." I hesitate. "She's just so… so…"

"Not me," says Mom.

"Well, yeah," I say. "Not you."

Mom plucks a dog hair off her slacks, and sighs. "It struck me on my last trip to London that I've been, well, missing out on something. Not only needing to see more of you, but – I don't know, something else. Something crazy. Does that make sense?"

"Yeah, Mom." My heart does a warm, electric flip-flop. Missing out on crazy stuff is something I totally understand.

"And Cleopatra is the craziest thing I've ever seen. But she's quality crazy, you know? Not pedigreed, of course, but real. And for some reason, which I will never be able to explain, I had to bring her home."

I look into Cleopatra's warm, dancing eyes. They pull me in and touch me, tingly and deep.

I slide over closer to Mom and give her a bear hug, sandwiching Cleopatra snugly between us. She stretches her tongue straight up, trying to lick both of our faces.

Mom looks at me. Happy. The mom I remember. Is this really my mom?

"Of course, she can't have puppies." She wrinkles her brow in horror. "Just think what puppies would do to this carpet."

I look down at the priceless oriental rug and laugh.

Yep. It's my mom.

The Ninth Dragon

JENNIFER KRAMER

The crumpled dragon had been a work of art. This one had been more detailed than most, with hundreds of intricate cuts designed to offset the shimmer of the iridescent paper and add a feeling of depth where the scaled tail curved backwards, as if the dragon was leaping from the paper.

I feel a pang of guilt, and unclench my fist. The dragon's head is torn, and the holes that had once been eyes have pulled apart. My cousin, Chin had probably worked on this cutting for hours, maybe days. It had taken seconds to destroy it. I'd simply curled my fingers around it, and squeezed.

"Susu, what have you done?"

Mama's voice is angry. I fight the urge to hide the paper behind me. The cat – or rather the dragon – is already out of the bag. Instead, I smooth it carefully against my lap with my hand, trying to fix it. But I can't, so I hold it out to her.

"I'm sorry, Mama. It ripped when I opened the envelope."

It was partly true. The tip of the tail stuck when I slid my finger across the seal. Yes, partly true, but only a very, very small part – maybe 3 percent, based on the size of the dragon. I guess that makes the other 97 percent a lie. But how can I explain what I've done? Mama won't understand.

The letter that came with the paper dragon is on the counter.

Dear Cousin Susu,

Guess what? Your mama has arranged for me to come and show my paper-cuttings at your local community centre for the Chinese New Year! I will be a featured artist! I have not been to the United States since I was a baby. Is it not exciting? Your mama says I can stay with you in your room. She says my dragons will be a hit!

We will be there on January 27th, and I'll be staying the whole week. Don't worry. I'll bring plenty of paper.

Love, Chin

PS I am enclosing a dragon. Have I sent one before? Some people consider them one of the harder cuttings to make, but for me they are simple.

The Chinese New Year has always been a special time for my family. Every year, for as long as I can remember, we have helped to plan the New Year events for the local Chinese Community Centre. While Papa and the other men build the stage and organise the parade, Mama and I have always handled the cooking, the cleaning and the decorating, together – just us.

It's the one time of year when I don't mind chores. I love wrapping the dumplings, filling the rice pots, steaming the sticky buns. I love hanging the streamers and the tapestries. I love sorting through the little red envelopes filled with "lucky money". And I love collecting the lanterns the younger kids have made and setting them along the parade path, saving the best to release in the river.

But most of all, I love the special time with Mama – just us.

So why did she invite my cousin? Doesn't she understand that this is *our* time? Or am I not enough? My answer is there in black and white, in that letter. Black, white and the colours of the rainbow that line each shelf and mantelpiece in our home with my cousin's paper-cuttings.

"That hardly explains this…" said Mama. For a moment, both her English and Chinese seem to desert her. She holds the dragon up to the light, and shakes her head. "You've destroyed it! How could you? How could you do this?"

"She can make another one."

The words seem weak even to me, but I don't know what else to say. My hands feel empty, and I cross them in front of me, as if they can defend what my words cannot. "Besides, it's only paper. That one was too — delicate."

"That's not the point!" Mama's chest rises with her voice. "And it's not just paper. It's art. More importantly, it's a gift, from your cousin! Each one is special. You know she never makes the same design twice. How could you be so careless?"

"But we already have — what — eight other dragons? And butterflies and horses and tigers and fish and flowers. They're everywhere! Doesn't she have anyone else to send them to?"

As soon as I say the words, I wish I could snatch them back. Mama's face is turning colours of its own, and I think I'd rather face all nine of Chin's dragons right now — even Sir Crump-a-lot. When Mama speaks, though, her voice is soft, yet somehow that is worse. Each word punctuates the air more than a hundred decibels.

"It doesn't matter that we have others. Chin sends them to us — she shares her beautiful art with us because she loves us. And what do you do? This senseless act of… Sometimes, I don't understand you! Sometimes, I wish you could be more like your cousin."

I've heard the words before, inside my head, but out loud they are worse than I imagined. Hot, salty tears burn my eyes. I turn my head and try to blink them away, unwilling to let Mama know how hurt I am. Suddenly, all I know is that I need to escape – to leave Mama and her words behind. When she puts down the crumpled dragon to read the letter, I take it and run.

In my room, I open my maths book and carefully press the dragon inside. I don't know why I'm careful now, but I am. When I am finished, I start on my maths assignment. The numbers blur, but it doesn't matter. Maths is my best subject, and I can calculate in my sleep. Working with numbers is easy, predictable – soothing. The answers are there, right in front of you, and once you work them out, they don't change. You can count on them.

I hear Mama's footsteps. She pauses at my doorway, but I force myself not to look up, to focus on the numbers. I hear her sigh and move away, unwilling to interrupt my schoolwork. When she is gone, I put my head down into my arms, hoping the darkness will block out our fight, block out her words. But it doesn't.

Instead, my mind goes back to the day Chin's first paper-cutting came in the post. My class had been working on snowflakes. I'd worked hard at mine — folding the white paper, snipping out tiny shapes, and opening it to see how the shapes repeated themselves around the paper. I'd folded the snowflake over and over, until it was almost too thick too cut, snipping away to see how many patterns I could make.

I'd been proud of that snowflake, and eager to show Mama. I'd pictured her face when she opened it. I'd pictured her showing it to family and friends. And I'd pictured her hanging it on the refrigerator, asking for more.

But at home, it wasn't at all like I'd imagined. Instead, I'd found something else already taped to the refrigerator, before I could even pull my carefully folded snowflake out of my backpack. "Come and see what your cousin Chin made! It's a paper-cutting. Do you see the two fish? It's like one I made when I was little, but so much better! Your cousin, she is wonderful! Talented!"

Compared to the crumpled dragon, it had been a simple cutting, but the two fish had made a pretty picture of flowing lines. More importantly, they'd been a symbol of something important to Mama. Something she remembered, and loved. Next to it, my snowflake had seemed to melt away —

just plain, holey paper. A doily.

A few days later, I'd made a pot holder. I'd used Mama's favourite colours, weaving the cloth loops in and out of the loom. But Chin had sent another paper-cutting. She'd used two-coloured paper, and folded it so the fish arched down, as if looking at its reflection in a pond.

"Tsst, tsst," Mama had said. "That girl, she is so creative. How does she think of such things? Mark my words, she has the hands of an artist."

And, of course, that wasn't the end. In the weeks that followed, my clay pinch-pot was met with Chin's paper tiger, my clothespeg butterfly with her lotus blossom, my lollipop-stick pencil-holder with her first dragon. With each letter, a new cutting, each more intricate and stunning than the last, as Chin progressed beyond symmetry and began working with layers and different types of paper.

Even in Taiwan, where paper-cutting is a traditional pastime, Chin's work had begun to attract the attention of artists, teachers, and reporters. Of course, her biggest fan has always been here, in my house. It is my mama, who tells everyone about her niece, the artist. It is my mama, who has saved every cutting, every letter, every article.

As for me, I've become good at maths.

And I've never made another snowflake.

❦ ❦ ❦

Einstein worked with something known as the Theory of Relativity. I have my own version. There is an inversely proportional relationship between the desirability of an event and the speed time travels towards that event, particularly when it comes to relatives. In other words, the more you can't wait for something to happen, the more you do. The less you want it to happen, the faster it does.

In this case, two weeks pass in the blink of an eye. I can hardly believe my cousin is here, in my house, my kitchen. I've seen pictures of her before, but for some reason I expected her to be bigger, more colourful. Instead, she looks very ordinary. She's wearing a tartan skirt, a white blouse, and brown shoes with gold buckles. Her hair is pulled back in a ponytail, and her hands are pushed into her skirt pockets.

Like Auntie Mae, she's tiny. It's hard to imagine her as a girl who cuts dragons. But I suppose I don't look much like a girl who crumples them.

"Hi," she says. "I'm Chin."

No, really? "Hi."

I should hold out my hand, but hers are dug deep into her pockets, and I don't want to stand there feeling foolish while she tries to pull them out.

One week – seven days. Just seven days.

Luckily, Mama and Auntie Mae have more than enough chatter between them to fill the room – and three others. I haven't seen Auntie Mae since I was a baby, and I don't think I've ever seen Mama like this. She is talking and arguing and laughing, all at once, like my friends and I do at school. But she's old, and it's a little embarrassing. Another reason to be glad this side of the family lives far away.

Uncle Po, who brought them from the airport, complains that his head hurts. "They used up all the oxygen in the car!"

Papa laughs, "Slow down, ladies. You have all week. Why don't Po and I take your suitcases upstairs, while you settle in?"

On the way out of the room, they wink at us. Uncle Po has a suitcase in one arm and a bag of pretzels in the other. Papa abandons any pretence of being helpful and follows with drinks. If only I could escape so easily.

"Do you want to go outside and skip?" I ask. "Or play hopscotch?"

Chin shakes her head. "No thank you, cousin."

Seven days – 168 hours. Just 168 hours.

Chin holds up a canvas bag. I see the handles of two pairs of scissors poking up from a side opening. "Do you want to see some of my paper-cuttings? I brought my book. And I have started a couple of new stencils. We can use them for the wall hangings and streamers…"

"Maybe later."

I should show an interest. Mama would expect it. After all, Chin is a guest in our house. More importantly, she's family. But she's only been here a few minutes, and already I feel like she's trying to change things. What's wrong with the streamers and balloons we use every year?

So we stand there, watching our mamas talk back and forth, and over and under. I wonder how they can hear one another, but I'm thankful they're so engrossed that they don't notice us. I like seeing Mama so happy and animated. I just wish it was for a different reason.

"Are you following this?" Chin asks at last, breaking the silence between us.

I shake my head. "No, are you?"

For the first time since she arrived, Chin smiles. Her lips turn up faintly, and her eyes crinkle. She shakes her head. "It's all Chinese to me."

Her response takes me by surprise. I can't help myself, and I laugh. After all, Chinese may be my second language, but it's Chin's first. My cousin has a sense of humour. The tension between us eases just slightly, but it's enough for me to regain my bearings, and my manners.

"Do you want to see my room?" I ask. "You can put down your stuff, and I can take you on a tour."

"Sure," says Chin. "Should we tell them?"

Mama and Auntie Mae are involved in a heated argument. Their wild arm-gestures and smiles show that they're enjoying every moment of it. There won't be any winner, and neither of them will care. Since they still haven't noticed us, I shake my head. "They'll work it out."

As we walk through the dining room, Chin seems impressed. "Your house is big."

"Big?" Our house is fairly average, at least compared to my friends' homes. I've never been to Chin's apartment in Taipei, but I remember Mama telling me that it is seven floors high. Because of the limited amount of land in the city, there's only one room on each floor. It's hard to imagine.

"Yes, very big," says Chin. "You are lucky to have only one flight of stairs!"

I remember how my PE teacher made us run up and down the bleachers last year, before soccer season. I hated it. The whole team hated it. How would it be if I had to climb four flights just to go to the lavatory? No wonder Chin is so small. She gets lots of exercise.

Just then, Chin stops. It's so quick that I almost crash into her. "Wow!"

She is looking around in wonder. From where we are, she can see the family room, where many of her paper-cuttings are lined up on the shelves. "My cuttings! You've saved them!"

She sounds surprised, even delighted. For me, it's just an unwelcome reminder. I follow her as she circles the room.

"Mama has saved every single one you sent." Well, except for the ninth dragon. That one is still in my maths book, a fraction of its old self.

Mama has a rule about keeping unkind thoughts to ourselves, and I am. But my earlier guilt fades as Chin picks up each of the colourful cuttings, as if she's never seen them before. "Oh, I remember this one! And this one! And here's the one I made when I was practising with pins."

One hundred and sixty-eight hours – 10,080 minutes. Just 10,080 minutes.

"You saved – all of them?" she asks.

"My mama has."

"But even my own mama, she does not save them all. She says there are too many – that I leave little bits of paper everywhere – that I make too many messes."

"My mama thinks your work is beautiful. She treats them as if they were gold. She wishes that I could be more like you." My voice is flat, dull.

Chin doesn't notice. "Really? Why, that's

wonderful!"

"Oh yes. Wonderful." Sarcasm now adds an angry edge to my tone, and Chin hears it.

Ten thousand and eighty minutes. Multiplied by sixty?

"No, no," said Chin. "You don't understand. My mama, she says the same things."

In the midst of carrying zeroes, I'm confused. "Auntie Mae? Why should she care if I'm like you?"

Chin giggles. "Not you, silly! Me. She wishes I was like you."

"Like me?" I parrot.

Chin nods. "Always, she tells me about the things you do. How you made the maths team at school, and kicked the winning goal at soccer, and played the piano for your talent show."

"Your mama knows about that?" I'm embarrassed, but pleased.

"Auntie Lucy tells her, of course."

"Auntie Lucy?" Lucy is Mama's name, but I'm not used to hearing her called that. "My mama tells… your mama?"

Now Chin has a funny look on her face. She speaks slowly, as if she doesn't think I'll understand, even though she's speaking English. "Yes, and it can be annoying, hearing about you all the time."

"Hearing about me?" Suddenly, I'm defensive.

"Look around you! I not only have to hear about you, my cousin, but I have to see your work every single day! Everywhere I turn!"

Chin's face flushes. She is offended. "I didn't realise you didn't like them!"

"It's not that," I say, though it's partly true. "You've sent so many, and, well…"

"I didn't know you were keeping them all," Chin admits. "Or that I'd sent so many. But I had to do something, to measure up to my American cousin."

"Measure up? To me?"

Chin is tiny, but I'm only a few inches taller. I smile. I don't think that anyone has ever tried to measure up to me before. It's a heady thought.

My cousin is still speaking. "My mama says that I should be more like you. More… well-rounded, more studious, more athletic. You know, more… *versile?*"

"Versatile?"

"Yes, that's the word. She says, 'Don't you want to play ball? Read a book? It is not good to do just one thing. You must be like your cousin Susu – good at many things. Useful things, like maths. Not just sitting at a table, going snip-snip-snip.'"

I'm stunned. "She says that?"

"All the time. So I tell her she must stop snip-snip-snipping at me. And after that, we do not talk to each other anymore, sometimes for the rest of the day. It is hard to take. Sometimes I have wished I didn't have an American cousin."

Chin flushes, as if she has just remembered who she is talking to, and that she is standing here, in my room. "But I didn't mean it – not really. Well, perhaps a tiny bit."

A tiny bit? Like that ninth dragon got a tiny bit – crumpled.

But I know exactly what she means.

A few minutes later, Auntie Mae and Mama join us. I am showing Chin pictures I have from the last New Year's parade.

"See?" beams Auntie Mae. "I told you our girls would get along."

"Of course," agrees Mama. "Like sisters."

Chin and I both roll our eyes. Then I take a deep breath. Since that day, two weeks ago, the ninth dragon has been burning a hole in my maths book. I haven't been able to fix him or throw him away. Now, I want him out of there, so I speak quickly, before I can change my mind.

"Mama, Chin's dragon – the one she sent two weeks ago? I ruined it, on purpose. I mean… a tiny bit was an accident, but most of it was on purpose."

Mama is surprised. I don't know if it's my words, or that I'm bringing it up now, so suddenly, in front of my cousin and aunt.

"But why? Why did you do it?"

"I was angry with you for inviting them!" I answer. "You didn't ask me! I thought preparing for the New Year was supposed to be our time. Yours and mine."

Mama looks confused. "And it still is. Perhaps we should talk about this later."

"No, Mama. I want to tell you now. I think Chin understands, at least a tiny bit. I was jealous. Of her, of her talent, of her art. Most of all, of how proud you are of her."

"But I am proud of you too!"

"Not the way you are of her. You talk about how she is talented and dedicated, how she makes beautiful things! Look around. You have her paper-cuttings everywhere. Not mine, hers."

"But you have not made any paper-cuttings!" says Mama, clearly exasperated. "And her work is beautiful. Of course I am proud of her. But I am no less proud of you. You are my daughter! I would not want you to be different."

"But you do," I remind her. "Remember? You said you wished I was more like her."

Mama looks puzzled. "I said that? I was angry that day. Sometimes we say things we don't mean when we are angry."

"And do things we don't mean to do," I say

quietly.

Mama puts her arm around me. "You are my daughter, and I am very proud of you. All the time. Well… most of the time."

Auntie Mae smiles. "Yes, you should hear how she speaks of you! I will show you my phone bill – then you will know how proud your mama is of you. And how proud I am, too. Ask Chin." Auntie Mae hugs my cousin. "And of course, I am proud of my own daughter, as well."

I wish I could see Chin's expression, but her face is hidden in Auntie Mae's shoulder.

"Your auntie Mae and I," says Mama. "We used to fight all the time, when we were younger."

"When you were younger?" Chin and I exchange a look, thinking about the scene in the kitchen.

"We were very competitive," agrees Auntie Mae. "We still are. But we are proud of each other now, too, and of you. Both of you."

"Now that we are apart, we miss each other very much," said Mama. "So perhaps I do talk about your cousin a lot. The competing was fun! But sometimes it was also hard. Your auntie Mae was good at many things!"

"Tsst, tsst," says Auntie Mae. She sounds like Mama. "Enough! We are a family. And we are all wonderful. Every last one of us. But right now, we have a party to plan! Let's go down and get to work."

After they leave, I turn to my cousin. "Are you angry about the dragon?"

"It did take me a long time to make that one," Chin answers. "But after all, it's only paper."

"No, it isn't." It feels strange to be defending her work. "You are very talented. And it was a great dragon. I'm sorry."

Chin is quiet for a moment. Then she smiles, "I know! I will make you a new one – to replace the dragon."

"That would be great," I say. "Thank you."

I don't mention that we have hundreds of other cuttings, including eight dragons, already. I am just grateful she knows what I did and has forgiven me. I wonder if this dragon will be like the last? I hope it will be a new dragon, like our new friendship.

As I watch, Chin pulls a sheet of lightly textured rice paper from her bag. Her hands fly over the thin sheet like hummingbirds, quick and sure as she turns and flip and folds. She uses no stencil, yet she cuts as if she already sees a picture of what it will be. Before I know it, she is gently separating the layers and folds. When she shows it to me, I am stunned.

It is beautiful. It is her best work ever. And it is not a dragon. It's a simple cutting, symmetrical like the fish she'd sent so long ago. It is two girls, hand-in-hand – cousins.

Mama calls from the kitchen. "Girls, come. We need you to taste the sauce for the sticky buns!"

"Yum," Chin and I say, together. I grin. I guess some sentiments are the same in English and Chinese. I put my new cutting on the shelf, next to my maths book.

"Perfect," I say. "Now for one of our family traditions. Last one down – eats a hundred-year-old duck egg!"

Chin makes a face. We both take off, running. After all, my cousin is only going to be here for a week.

And we don't want to miss a second of it.

The Surprise

Jenny Land

"Is Marlene Whittaker in class today? She has a message at the main office."

The grey-haired secretary shut the classroom door again, never noticing my grimace at my desk as my classmates smirked at her use of my old-fashioned full name. My friend Julia shot me a sympathetic glance. Why, I asked myself, had my mother ever given me such a curse? Even if it had been her own mother's name?

"Marlie?" Mr Nibley came over to my desk, where I had markers spread out to work on my history project. "It's all right, you can get the message now. If it's your mother, tell her I said hi."

He winked at me, and I almost felt like winking back. All of us loved Mr Nibley, or "Mr N" as he was known affectionately; he was one of those rare teachers who never made you sit still for more than five minutes, and who actually made history fun. We did a skit one time where Julia and I wore wigs as James Madison and Thomas Jefferson; I couldn't possibly forget what the Constitution said after that. Plus, Mr Nibley, of all people, understood how hard it was to have a name people laughed at.

"No problem, Mr N," I told him, and headed down the narrow, fluorescent-lit corridor to the principal's office.

Sure enough, the note asked me to call back my mother straightaway.

"Hi Mom," I said, holding the phone at the corner of the secretary's desk.

"Marlie, is that you?"

"Who else calls you Mom?" I couldn't help laughing. I pictured Mom at home, in her studio off the dairy barn, still in sandals despite the November chill, adamant that it was still too early to fire up the woodstove. I could imagine dabs of wild-coloured paints decorating not only the canvas, but also her hands and strands of her greying ponytail.

"Look, Marlie, I know you're out of class, so I'll cut to the chase. What do you have eighth period?"

"French."

"Do you have a test, or some special project?"

"No…"

"Good. Meet me out front at 1.30. I've got a surprise for you."

"You mean you want me to…" my voice trailed off as I almost said, "cut class?" Mercifully, the secretary's keys kept clicking away, so it didn't matter.

"You bet, leave school," my mother finished for me. "See you then."

Mom's voice echoed in my ear as I handed the phone back to the secretary, who listened to my mother and filled out an absence-excuse slip for me to take to my French teacher next class. The secretary didn't seem to notice my beetroot-red face, and I hurried back down the corridor as soon as I could.

Back in the classroom, I couldn't help staring at the clock. What could Mom possibly want? History class crawled, and my mind raced over all sorts of possibilities. Over everything, that is, except the rise of the cotton gin in the South, and I soon realised I'd have to concentrate on finishing my Civil War board-game as homework instead of in class.

Something seemed strange about Mom calling me like that. It wasn't like her to let me miss school for anything. She was one of those parents who arranged your dentist appointment after school so you didn't miss anything important. She always quizzed me on my pre-algebra equations the night before a test, until even a maths dimwit like me couldn't completely mess up. *It must be something horribly important,* I told myself. But what? She hadn't seemed anxious or upset, had she? In fact, she'd sounded decidedly cheerful – even conspiratorial.

After class, I hurriedly packed up my bag and grabbed my coat from the hall, avoiding Julia so I wouldn't have to explain anything. I dashed down to the French classroom to let the teacher know I had to miss class. Then I came back to the lobby and sat on the bench nearest to the corner, trying to look as inconspicuous as possible, as though I were just one of those kids heading off to a doctor's appointment. I waited long enough to realise that I probably could have attended a good chunk of French class: true to form, Mom arrived a quarter of an hour late.

"Sorry, honey," she told me blithely, kissing my cheek as I crawled up into the passenger seat of our blue Ford pickup truck. Sure enough, her old pair of jeans had little flecks of paint of every colour on them. "I forgot Lew Brown had an appointment over in Ashton today," she went on, "so I had to milk the girls on my own. Oh! And Marlie, I had a real breakthrough on the Red Gate painting... The whole thing should be set at dusk, don't you think? So I painted out the yellow." Mom carried on in a decidedly chirpy tone; nothing could be wrong, at least, I told myself.

Although Mom was still firmly enmeshed in art-world notions, I only half-listened, and noticed her turn left at the stop sign, away from home, north out onto Route 7.

I finally interrupted her. "Mom, where are you taking me?"

Mom absently tucked some stray hairs behind her ears and adjusted the radio, switching from the classical station to one that blared out some bluegrass. "Oh, you'll see. Better not tell you in case it doesn't work out for some reason. Down by Starkville," she added vaguely. "Did you get the homework from your last class?"

"Yes, Mom," I sighed, staring out at the bare and rolling cornfields, now harvested down to the brown stubs. The late-autumn colours actually had a mellow prettiness, but I longed for winter. It just had to snow soon. "Hey, I forgot, your pal Mr N said to say hi," I added, giggling a bit. Mom hadn't treated a man seriously in my memory, and to the best of my knowledge hadn't had one more than just passing through ever since Dad left the picture when I was a baby. "Where did you go on that date with him, Mom? The dance at the Grange hall?"

"That was our first date, yes. I've seen him more than once since then."

My mom? Dating my teacher? This was certainly news to me. An evening out with someone was one thing; I'd grown used to that. I even liked to see with whom she'd head out for dinner next, and how she'd fix herself up. She always assured me that the lavender bath salts I gave her on her birthdays were definitely the key ingredient to a successful night out, given that she was a dairy farmer. But this sounded different; more than one date meant serious business. I couldn't help thinking back to school in the past few months, and wondered how this turn of events might have shaped my time in the classroom. Mr N must have been thinking of my mother whenever he saw me. Out loud, I couldn't help saying, "Mom, he's my teacher – you didn't even know him before parent–student conference day." Then I thought, *What if she marries him? Would she change her last name to Nibley? Would I have to?* "When have you been seeing him, anyway?" I asked, as casually as possible.

Mom slowed for a traffic light in Lanesboro village, and looked over at me with consternation. "I haven't meant to hide anything at all from you, Marlie." She paused. "Well, it's been too soon, too uncertain maybe, to say anything. Besides, it seems like we haven't had a good long talk lately. I suppose you've been away quite a bit."

This was true, I admitted to myself. I'd spent October break on a school trip down in Boston, and my friend Julia and I had been building an elaborate treehouse at her place ever since September. I stared out at the austere grey stone buildings of Timory College in the little town we were passing through. It seemed impossible that I hadn't noticed anything new with Mom — I'd just seen her doing the same old things, working in the barn and the pasture with Lew, snatching moments in her studio when she could.

"Well, here's the road," Mom announced, turning left along a paved road that cut between two farms. Enormous cornfields spread out on either side of the road, and we headed towards the lake that divided us from New York State. The mountains across on the other side looked almost close enough to touch.

I recognised the turn immediately. "Mom, this is just the road out to that llama farm."

Mom started to laugh. "You have a good memory! I forgot I'd taken you along that day I checked it out. That was summer, though, and this is an autumn trip. We won't need to drive out quite that far, anyhow."

The fields looked as drab as the smouldering grey clouds rising above them, as dark as the lead-coloured strip of lake that lay beyond. Why on earth had Mom taken me out of school to visit a farm by the lake?

Then, gradually, I became aware of a buzzing sound through the draughty windows of the pickup. And then honks. Craning my neck so I could see upwards, above the windscreen, I saw an enormous V of geese fly by, and then another close behind, each with well over a hundred birds. They flew so low I could make out the flapping of wings, and the second V appeared to merge into the first, making the most enormous formation of birds I'd ever seen.

"Did you see that, Mom?"

Mom nodded with a grin. She pulled left across the road to the field on the opposite side, onto a farm track that ended at a sturdy fence. Mom parked and tossed me an old army coat that had belonged to Dad, one that I wore at home a lot to help with chores. "Your scarf is tucked inside the arm, Marlie." She hopped out and went to the fence edge. She balanced her elbows on the top rail and attempted to focus a pair of ancient binoculars.

I got out and stood next to her, looking past the stumpy, clipped rows of corn towards what appeared to be a second lake, almost white, shimmering. Maybe the field had flooded. I could still hear the honking, louder than before. Mom handed me the binoculars, and as I peered through and adjusted them, I could see that the shimmering white was not water at all, but a really huge flock of birds — thousands of them, pecking at the ground, rising and hovering, and then slowly settling again. Their honking sounded beautifully wild in the emptiness of the huge grey sky.

"Snow geese," Mom told me triumphantly, looking out towards the flock. "They come here every year, just for a short while, and I always used to come down here as a kid with my mom. You know, the Marlene you're named for. She always loved birds of any kind."

I looked at Mom quietly, at her grey hair blowing in the November wind, and wondered how she'd looked at my age, or even younger, standing here next to the other Marlene.

"This is also the place your father proposed to me," Mom said, her voice low, almost as if she wasn't talking to me but to herself. She jammed her hands into the pockets of her quilted jacket and stared out at the field. "I suppose I never quite thought of taking you here – too many memories. But lots of good memories, too, when I think about it. And I thought you'd like the geese."

She turned to me with a worried expression, as if she thought I might be upset, but I smiled back in reassurance, and looked back out at the geese, because I didn't know what to say, but I also couldn't stop looking. I almost thought that I should hug her, but we didn't do that much, except before and after times apart, and the moment passed. I thought she knew how I felt anyhow, even though I stayed quiet.

Leaving the binoculars at my side, I looked out instead at the indistinct blur of pure whiteness, every now and then watching a group of birds rise above the ground, hover a bit, and then lower again. Occasionally the group would rise up even higher and fly up towards the clouds, perhaps seeking out the other birds in formation. I wondered where in the south the geese were heading, and what far northern land they'd left behind. I liked knowing that they'd been here before, and that they'd come back again, always to the same place.

"So the geese always come here, even when we can't," I said out loud.

"Yes, something like that," Mom replied quietly. She paused and then added, "I hope you didn't mind me taking you out of school like that today, Marlie. I'm sorry, maybe it wasn't such a good idea. I didn't even ask; do you have plans with Julia after school?"

I handed the binoculars back to Mom and smiled at her again. "No, nothing at all. Except that Mr N might be hoping for a phone call from you later on."

Mom started to laugh, her warm breath rising in a curl of white steam above her in the cold, and I almost couldn't hear the sound of it for all of the honking.

"Later, Marlie," she said, reaching along the fence and pulling me into the fold of her coat. "It's just our day for now."

"Mom," I whispered up towards her, "Is it OK if we come every year? Whatever happens?"

"Whatever happens," Mom told me. "You and me."

Mum Never Did Learn to Knock

CATHY HOPKINS

There was a hammering on the bathroom door. "Emily, who are you talking to in there?" called Dad.

"Speak later, Mum. Don't worry, I'm on the case. I'll find out what I can," I whispered into my mobile phone, then quickly flipped it shut. I opened the bathroom door giving my best innocent smile. "No one. Just cleaning my teeth."

Dad didn't look convinced. "I heard you," he insisted. "You were talking to your mother again, weren't you?"

"No."

"Well, you were talking to someone. I heard you."

I waved my phone at him. "Lou. I was talking to Lou, that's all," I said. "Homework thingee. So, what's for supper?" *Change the subject fast,* I thought, as Dad's expression showed concern. "Take-away or take-away? I fancy pizza. Four cheeses. OK?"

We've lived on take-aways since Mum left. I did attempt to cook at first, but wasn't too good at it besides cheese on toast, and Dad can only do rubbery scrambled eggs. Yuck.

Dad put his hand on my shoulder. "Emily… would you… would you like to talk to someone?"

"Someone?"

"A counsellor."

"Why? Like who? Not Aunt Iz, *puleese*. She lives in wacko land."

Aunt Iz is Dad's barmy younger sister and calls herself a new-age counsellor. All kinds of people go to her for healing-schmealing, and she consults the Tarot and stars on their behalf and advises them to drink disgusting-tasting herbs. So, Aunt Iz? No, ta. Mum and I used to joke that she was a witch.

"No, no, I mean a proper counsellor," said Dad. "There are people who specialise in… well, situations like ours."

So now he thinks I need help, I thought. *Just because I've stayed in touch with Mum. I wish he'd see her or talk to her at least. She's looking great now. Loads better than before she left. Dad's the one that ought to see a counsellor. He's the one who's bottled everything up and thrown himself into his work so that he doesn't have to think about what happened.*

"No thanks, Dad," I said. "I'm fine. And I'll… I've stopped talking to her." *Liar, liar, pants on fire,* I thought, *but what else am I to do? I'm not having people thinking I'm bonkers, just because I want to talk to my mum.*

Dad looked at the floor and shifted awkwardly. "It's not just me, Em," he said. "Miss Doolie phoned from the school last night. They're worried about you there, too. Said you've been behaving strangely – and it seems that you saw your mother at school."

Well, I'm not likely to turn her away, I thought, *not now that she needs me.*

"Miss Doolie has arranged for you to see the school counsellor on Monday at lunchtime…"

"Oh Da-ad. Gimme a break. I told you, I've stopped talking to her, so I don't see what the problem is. Look, no way do I need to see a counsellor. That's for saddos."

Dad pressed my shoulder. "Do it for me, kid. I know these past weeks have been tough on you."

❦ ❦ ❦

It won't be so bad, I told myself the following Monday as I set off to see the counsellor. *She's probably one of those old hippie types like Aunt Iz, all long, flowing Afghan skirts and big ethnic beads. I'll just say what she wants to hear and have her eating out of my hand.* Aunt Iz was a pushover as long as you agreed to be open-minded and let her wave a crystal or two over you.

As I sat waiting in the corridor, Mark Riley and Andrew Derrington walked past.

"All right, Potts?" called Andrew. "In to see the shrink, are you? What've you done? Wet your bed? Gone potty? Hey that's good, Emily Potts has gone potty."

"Get lost, potato head," I replied with as much disdain as I could muster. "Actually, I'm here because they're thinking of transferring me to a school for gifted pupils. They're worried that my natural talent is being held back because I have to mix with bozos like you."

Mark cracked up. He fancies me, I know he does. He told Avril Jeffries in Year 9 and she told Lou, and Lou told me. And he's OK for a boy. Cute-looking with no spots. He laughs easily, too. I like that.

"You, gifted? Yeah, right," said Andrew. "You definitely need help."

At that moment, my mobile bleeped and luckily the boys moved off so I could answer. It was Mum.

"Hey, Emily, sorry I haven't been in touch since Saturday. I'm still trying to adjust, you know…"

"I've been summoned to see a counsellor, Mum. Everyone thinks I'm losing the plot because of you, so I'm going to have to be cool about talking to you from now on… A lot of people don't understand."

"Funny, isn't it? If anyone needs a counsellor at the moment," she said, "it's me. No one prepares you for this, and I really don't know what I'm supposed to do next. It was so easy with your father. He always knew what to do."

"So why haven't you tried talking to him?"

"Oh I have," she snorted. "Don't think I haven't tried, but he's not receptive. He just blanks me. It's like I've become invisible to him."

"His way of dealing with it. You know how he likes to compartmentalise things. That was then, this is now kind-of-thing."

"I know, love," she said. "Thank God I still have you."

The door opened and the school secretary stuck her head out.

"You can go in now, Emily. Mrs Armstrong is waiting."

"Catch you later," I said to Mum as I got up and flipped my phone shut.

Inside the room was dingy and it smelt musty, like no one had opened the windows in years. Around a battered-looking coffee table were three chairs that looked like they'd come off a skip, one orange, one brown and one flowery – and on top of the table was a large box of tissues. *People must do a lot of crying in here,* I thought as a tall, white-haired lady got up to greet me.

"You must be Emily Potts," she said as she offered me her hand.

I nodded. I'd give my name away, but nothing else.

"Take a seat," she said, pointing at a chair.

I did as I was told and sat opposite her.

"I'm Mrs Armstrong," she said, "but you can call me Gloria."

She was nothing like I expected. She was wearing a navy-blue, tailored suit with high heels. She looked more like a business lady than a touchy-feely-type helper out to heal the world.

"You the counsellor?" I asked.

She nodded. "I am. Is that OK?"

I shrugged. "I guess."

She glanced down at a book of notes, then back up at me. "So, Emily, let's get down to business," she said. "Now. Do you want to tell me a little about yourself?"

No, but I thought I'd better make some kind of effort. Hmm. What to say to keep her off the Mum trail?

"Um. Usual," I said. "Five foot two at the last count but still growing, I hope. Medium build. Wish I was taller, wish I was thinner. I like art and English. Don't like the colour of my hair. Dad calls it chestnut, but I think it's boring and I'd like some highlights, but he won't let me. Dunno. Usual stuff."

Gloria didn't seem that interested, but she made a few notes in her book, then looked back up at me.

"Yes. I can see what you look like, Emily. What I meant to ask is, what's been going on with you lately?"

I shrugged again. "Nothing. Same old, same old."

"Talking of which, how old are you exactly?"

"Exactly? Er…" I had to think for a moment. "Twelve years, three months… er… four days…" I glanced at my watch, "twelve hours and about ten minutes. Exactly."

Gloria didn't smile. "I see," she said and made another note in her book. "So… why do you think you've been sent to see me?"

I shrugged. "Dunno."

"OK, so how do you feel about seeing me?"

"Dunno. OK I suppose." Silence from Gloria so I thought I'd better add something. "How do you feel about seeing me?"

"I feel good about seeing you," said Gloria in a soft voice that made me feel like throwing up. *Why do people feel they have to be quiet around me now and treat me with kid gloves? It's not like what's happened is a first.* "But I'm concerned. Your teachers told me about your mother."

"Have they?"

"They have," said Gloria followed by another long silence.

"What about her?"

Gloria coughed and shifted in her seat. "That she... she died three weeks ago."

"Yeah. So?"

"Well, I'm told that you talk to her. I know, nothing wrong with that. A lot of people in your situation do, but you do know that she's dead, don't you?"

Another looooong silence. I wondered if I was supposed to pitch in, or if she was waiting for me to break down and cry – hence the tissues.

It was Gloria who cracked and spoke first. "I wonder... how do you feel about that?" she asked, in a voice so soft you could hardly hear her.

I felt like laughing. *How do I feel about that? Oh, over the moon, Gloria. It's great to see your mum fade away in front of you. Best time of my life. Not.*

"How do you think I feel?" I asked, carefully omitting the words *you dingbat* that I was thinking.

"Are you aware that you keep asking me questions, Emily?"

"Are you aware that you keep asking *me* questions, Gloria?" I mean, asking if I knew Mum was dead, and how did I feel about it – I thought, *How stupid can you get? Of course I know Mum's dead. I was at her funeral.* OK, it didn't sink in right away, as before that she'd always been there, every day, since I was born. I know that's obvious, but not everybody in your life has been there all the time from the start.

It didn't seem real when she died. Couldn't be true. Like she'd gone to the hospital for a few days and would walk back in through the door at any moment. At first I took Dad's attitude – kept myself busy, tried to cook a bit, cleaned the house, did the washing and stuff. Tried to shut out the enormity of it. It wasn't like her death was unexpected. She'd been ill for almost a year and we'd had long chats about how it would be when she'd gone. She was so organised about it all. Even down to choosing the music, flowers and readings for her funeral. She was like that, Mum. Mrs Efficient.

Then, one day, it hit me that she really wasn't coming back this time. I was in the downstairs cloakroom and it still smelt of her perfume. She always kept a bottle down there. Ô de Lancome. Light. Lemony. I realised that the scent would fade as Mum had. I sat on the loo and reached for a piece of toilet paper, only to find that the roll had finished and there wasn't any more in the cupboard under the sink where she usually kept it. It was then that it hit home. My mum really had gone. There was no one to buy the loo rolls anymore. There was no one to take care of me anymore.

I sat there and sobbed my heart out. It felt like a dam burst inside me, and all the feelings I'd been holding back came flooding out, bringing with them a thousand questions. And the biggest one was, where had she gone? I realised that in all the chats we'd had about her dying and about me coping afterwards, she'd never once mentioned where she would be going. I couldn't believe we hadn't discussed it. She always left a note stuck on the fridge door when she went anywhere, even out to the shops for ten minutes. I went into the kitchen to double check. But no, nothing. Only a Santa magnet from last Christmas. I opened the back door and yelled with all my strength into the night sky, "WHERE ARE YOU? MUM! WHERE HAVE YOU GONE?"

A curtain twitched next door and I heard a window open so I whispered it again, *Where have you gone?* I kept asking myself over and over again, *Where do people go when they die?* So when Gloria asked if I realised that she was dead, the answer was *Yes, oh most definitely, yes.*

Gloria was still staring at me, waiting for me to say something, or break down, but I'd had enough. There was nothing Gloria could say or do to bring Mum back properly. One thing I knew for sure, though, and that was that I didn't want to be coming to counselling every week for the next month. I had to bluff my way out.

"So, this talking to your mother…" Gloria started.

"Listen, Mrs Arm – Gloria," I said. "Yes, I do talk to Mum. It makes me feel better, like she can hear me somewhere, wherever she is. Like she's not really gone. I'm not mad or disturbed or anything. I'm cool. I know she's dead."

Gloria looked at me sympathetically. "It must have been very hard for you."

I nodded. "Yeah." I wanted out of there to hang out with Mark. After assembly this morning, he'd asked what I was doing at lunchtime and even hinted that we could walk home together. "But I'm OK, I've got my dad. And Mum told me she'd be watching over me and I could always talk to her. That's why I do it. I'm not luni-petuni or anything. I'll be OK. I'm coping."

Gloria nodded and made a few notes on her pad. I think I had her convinced that I wasn't out of my mind, and she was just getting ready to round up our session, when Mum came in through the door. And I mean literally, right through the door. Cool, that.

"All right, love?" she asked as she hovered behind Gloria.

I nodded and motioned her to be quiet. Not that Gloria would see or hear her. Seems like it's only me that does that, but I didn't want to react or anything. I didn't want Gloria clocking that I wasn't just *talking* to Mum; I could *see* her. If Gloria thought that, then she'd definitely think I was unhinged and I'd have to come back to counselling another time.

"I was just thinking," said Mum, as Gloria put her notebook into her bag, "could you ask her if she knows where I'm supposed to go?"

"Um, Gloria, just one more thing," I said as Gloria got up.

Gloria smiled and sat again. "Yes, Emily."

"Er… where do people go when they die? I mean, where will Mum be? What happens when you die?"

Gloria paled. "Er, well… that's a big question."

"I know. Do you know the answer?"

Gloria looked at her watch. "I'm afraid we're out of time Emily. Er. So many big questions in life… let me get back to you on that."

Mum sat next to me and we both studied Gloria, hoping that she was going to say something. After a while, Mum shook her head. "I don't think she knows, love."

"Neither do I," I said.

"Pardon?" said Gloria.

"Oh. Nothing. Was just thinking, neither do I know where they go. Can I go now?"

Gloria nodded. "Unless there's anything else."

I couldn't resist. "Just one more question, if you don't mind."

Gloria was beginning to look distinctly worried. "Go ahead."

"What's after space?"

Mum burst out laughing, as it was the question I used to drive her mad with when I was in junior school.

Gloria looked like she couldn't wait to get out of the room. "My, but you're a curious child," she said and made another note on her pad. "Er. Can I get back to you on that as well?"

"Sure," I said. "Take all the time you need."

Gloria got up and hurried out of the room.

"Seems like nobody knows," said Mum when she'd gone.

"Seems like. Sorry, Mum, but I told you, I'll do my best to find out."

After the meeting with Gloria, Mum hung around for the rest of the afternoon. It was a blast, especially when she peeked at Mr Parker's notes, then gave me all the answers for my history test. It will be the first time ever that I get an A. After school, she didn't seem to be in a hurry to be off anywhere, and who could blame her, as she didn't know where to go. She said she needed to be around someone she knew, and no way was she hanging out at the cemetery where she was buried. "There's dead people in there," she said, then we both cracked up laughing.

It was brilliant having her around, and we joked about the fact that we spent more time together now she was dead than when she was alive. And it was easy to talk to her without attracting attention, as I simply got my phone out and pretended I was talking to someone on the other end. The rest of the week, we did the mall and went to a film, where Mum realised that there were some perks to being a ghostie as she got in without paying. We went to the library; she even sat at the back of most of my classes at school. It was hard not bursting out laughing at some points, when she shouted out answers to questions and humphed loudly if a teacher said anything she didn't approve of.

I did try to confide in my best mate, Lou, but she didn't want to know. I think she's gone into the "Emily has lost the plot" camp, no matter how much I tell her that it's cool. She's terrified of ghosts.

"Mum says ghosts aren't scary," I told her. "They're the same as normal people…"

"D'er, yeah, only one small difference," said Lou, "like, they're dead."

She wasn't having any of it. It's probably because she watches so many horror films, so she thinks that ghosts are all terrifying. I know different now. Mum said that just because you die, you don't have a personality change. She says it's fear, fear of the unknown that scares people. *Scares ghosts, too,* I thought but she's right about it being the unknown. It's weird. Death happens to everyone, and yet no one wants to talk about it, and no one really seems to know what happens.

Not that I wasn't scared when Mum first showed up. I was terrified. I was in the bath, the night after I'd been shouting my lungs out in the back garden, and suddenly she came floating out of the airing cupboard. Just like that. Dressed just how she used to be in real life, her old blue tracksuit and trainers. My first reaction was to scream and close my eyes to make her go away, but when I opened them, there she was, sitting on the edge of the bath, and my curiosity got the better of me, not having met a dead person before. When I realised that she wasn't going to rip her arm off and hit me with the soggy end, or spew green sick or anything wacko like that, we got talking. And that's when the trouble started and people began to think that I was disturbed and wasn't accepting her death. Of course, I knew it wasn't that. I knew she was dead and wasn't coming back how she was before. But she was there in another form, no doubt about that, and she needed my help.

Sadly, our research into the afterlife only seemed to confuse things. There was a wealth of material out there – sites on the Internet, books and magazines from the wonderful to the weird. Priests, gurus, philosophers, mystics, rabbis, all with their opinion-sminions.

"What we need," said Mum, as she picked up a book on world religions in the library, "is a sort of guide book. An A-Z of the afterlife sort of thing."

"Probably have it in WH Smith's," I joked. "They sell maps. If not, we could always go back to the Internet and type 'afterlife maps' into Google."

But we found nothing really useful anywhere — zilch. I didn't care. It was great having her around.

One night after school, Mark was waiting for me by the bus stop.

"All right, Potts?"

"Yeah. You?"

"Yeah."

Hmm. So far, a fascinating conversation — not, I thought and decided to take the plunge.

"Hey, Riley. You believe in ghosts?"

"I would if I saw one, but I haven't, so can't say."

"But you don't *not* believe?"

"No. Who knows? Why you seen one?"

"Yeah. My mum."

"Get out of here. When?"

"All the time. She's always popping up."

"She all green and slimy?"

I sighed. Another person who wasn't taking me

seriously. "No," I said. "She looks like Mum. But see-through. She smells different though. Not like her old perfume anymore. Her smell always arrives a moment before she does. It's divine, like a garden of roses in summer."

"Way to go, Potts. She around now?"

"No, but she probably will be later – that is, if she's not gone to see a film."

Mark looked at me as if I was mad. I guess it did sound a bit strange. Not your usual conversation with a boy you fancy. But then he smiled. "Why not?" he said. "Yeah. Cool."

"So you don't think I'm mad?"

He shook his head. "No. I've often wondered where people go when they die. My dog Petra died last year. It was awful. I mean, I know she was only a dog, but she was like my best mate. I'd had her all my life. She always slept on the end of my bed. And then she wasn't there anymore. I read everything I could about what happens next. Read up a lot about ghosts."

"So why do they stay around? I've been checking it out on the Net, but everyone seems to contradict each other."

"Apparently," said Mark, "ghosts hang around for two reasons. One, they died in a traumatic way and are in shock, like they haven't quite adjusted to the fact they're dead…"

"That's not Mum. She knew she was dying for about a year."

"And two, unfinished business."

"Like what?"

"Dunno. Left the oven on. Something not said or done. Something to clear up with someone still down here. Feeling responsible for someone they've left. So why do you reckon your ma's still around?"

I shrugged, but I was beginning to have an inkling.

🦋 🦋 🦋

"What exactly did happen when you left your body?" I asked Mum later that evening, when she turned up in my bedroom.

"Oo, it was lovely," she said. "I'd been drifting up a tunnel and floated out at the end into an ocean of white light. I felt surrounded by love and warmth. It felt like going home. I can't ever remember feeling so at peace. Then, suddenly, I had this terrible feeling that I'd forgotten something. Before I knew it, I felt myself being tugged earthwards, and found myself coming through the bathroom wall, and there you were. In the buff, in the bath."

"I know. You never did learn to knock," I said.

Mum grinned. "I would have if I could," she said, putting her hand through the wall for emphasis.

"I… I think I know why you came back. It was

me crying out for you. It was when I realised that you'd really gone. I felt such an overpowering sense of being alone, I was devastated. I think I brought you back. I was shouting out *Where are you?* as you'd forgotten to tell me where you were going. And I really missed you... and I wanted you back... I... I didn't know at the time what would happen."

Mum tried to put her arm round me, but it kept going through me, so she held it a few inches away, as though she was giving me a hug.

"I know, love. I'm sorry I couldn't let you know. Just... I didn't know at the time. But it seemed that I was going somewhere very nice. It really felt... oh, I can't describe it, but it was a good place." Then her face clouded, which is a strange look on someone who's transparent. Like a glass bowl that's steamed up. "But now I fear I might have missed the boat, or the ride, or whatever it was."

"No. It can't be like that. Like boarding a plane and if you miss your flight, you can't go. It can't be."

Mum shrugged. "Ah well. No doubt it will get sorted. So what are we doing tonight?"

"Ah..." Mark was coming over and I was hoping to see him on his own. I had a feeling that he wanted to kiss me but he didn't want to do it in front of her, and who could blame him? Dead or alive, having your mother as an audience for a first kiss is uncool in anyone's book.

Luckily, I was saved from hurting Mum's feelings by someone ringing the doorbell downstairs.

"It's your aunt Iz," Dad called up the stairs a few moments later.

"Maybe you'd better go," I said to Mum as she looked out of the window, hoping for a glimpse of Dad's sister.

"No way," she said. "I wouldn't miss this for the world."

We made our way downstairs, me walking, Mum floating behind me like Mary Poppins, and we found Aunt Iz in the kitchen. She'd brought a dish of orange gloop which she put on the table.

"A nice healthy lentil roast," she said, when she saw me looking. "I was worried you weren't eating properly."

Mum pulled an I'm-going-to-be-sick face behind her. She'd never liked Aunt Iz's cooking either.

Over supper, we chatted about school and talked a little about Mum's death. I had a really hard time keeping a straight face, as all the time, Mum was looning about the kitchen making mad faces and doing her impersonation of an Egyptian sand dancer in the air. That did it. I sprayed a mouthful of lentils everywhere and almost choked. I think Aunt Iz thought my hysteria was down to me being seriously disturbed about Mum's passing, so when we'd cleared away the dishes, she suggested we have a seance to try and contact Mum, so that she could reassure me that she was OK. She roped Dad in too. At first he was reluctant, as he's not into any of that heebie-jeebie stuff as he calls it, but I talked him round and he agreed, if only to stop Aunt Iz fussing.

We lit candles, sat at the kitchen table, and after a few minutes, Aunt Iz started swaying and rolling her eyeballs.

I had to bite my cheeks to stop myself from laughing, and I could see Dad trying not to smile.

"I think... I'm... m-making contact," said Aunt Iz in a strange deep voice as Mum floated past and stuck a finger up her nose.

Of course, that set me off again and my shoulders started to shake with suppressed laughter. And then Dad got the giggles, even though he couldn't see what was really going on. Mum was on a roll. She floated in and out through the pantry door. Then she'd disappear altogether and just stick her leg through then back again, then her arm in and out, then finally, her bum. By this time, I was on the floor laughing which soon snapped Aunt Iz out of her trance. And Dad had tears of laughter rolling down his cheeks at the sight of me desperately trying to keep it together and failing miserably.

"If neither of you is going to take me seriously, I'm leaving," she said, then stomped off and out the front door in a huff.

After she'd gone, Dad and I looked at each other. "More lentils, dear?" he sniggered.

"No, ta," I said, and we burst out laughing again.

Dad looked sad for a moment. "I think your mum would have enjoyed that," he said.

I put my hand over his. "Maybe she was watching us from wherever she is," I said.

"Maybe," Dad said softly.

Mum winked at me from behind him, then let her hand hover gently on his shoulder.

For a few weeks, we continued to have fun, but the novelty of seeing Mum appear and disappear was beginning to wear thin. I was seeing more and more of Mark. And that was the problem. Mum kept popping up at inappropriate moments to ask awkward questions:

"How long have you known this boy?"

"Aren't you a little young for a relationship?"

"Are you serious about him?"

We could never get any time on our own.

And the lack of privacy was beginning to get to me, like her coming out of the bath plug when I was in the bath, or out of my knicker drawer when I was getting changed. Or nudging me awake early in the morning because she was bored and wanted someone to talk to.

In the meantime, Mark helped me do my research into the afterlife. It seemed that a lot of people had had after-death experiences like Mum's when their heart had stopped on the operating table, or they'd had a car accident, or something, but they'd later come round to tell the tale. All of them seemed happy about dying since their near-death experience – in fact, some said they were quite looking forward to it when it happened properly, as they no longer had qualms that there wasn't somewhere wonderful to go to. Most of them said that they now believed that the physical body was nothing more than a shell that houses the real self. And Mum had to agree. She had no worries about going "back up there" either.

One night after school, Mark and I walked home through the park and we stopped at the old elm tree near the railings.

He put his arms around me and I snuggled in.

"Is she around?" he asked.

I sniffed the air for her rose smell and shook my head.

He tilted my chin up and leaned in to kiss me. *Get ready to pucker*, I thought as I glanced over his shoulder to make sure that there weren't any nosy neighbours around, ready to report back to Dad.

Suddenly the air filled with roses and Mum appeared on the other side of the railings.

I leapt back.

"What's up?" asked Mark. "Don't you want to?"

"No. Just…"

"Ah. Your mum showed?"

I nodded. "Muuum…" I began.

Mum looked particularly radiant. "Won't be a minute, sunshine," she said. "Just wanted to check you're all right."

"Yeeesss, I'm fine," I said, rolling my eyes. "Look, Mum, much as I love you, you can't keep popping up everywhere unannounced. I do have my own life you know and… bit of a private moment here…"

"I know, love," she said softly. "We've both got to move on. And… well… I… I think I'm ready to go now."

She smiled at me and gently brushed my cheek with her hand. Part of me wanted to yell *Noooooo, not yet, just a little longer,* but I knew it was time. I had to let her go. I smiled back and nodded.

And then she was gone. I inhaled the last lingering scent of roses as Mark wrapped me in his arms.

I never did see her again. But I still talk to her sometimes, and I'm sure she can hear me, wherever she's gone. And I don't feel worried anymore, as I'm sure it's someplace good.

And sometimes, just sometimes, like on my birthday, or days that for some reason I have the blues, I smell the scent of roses and know that she's not too far away. She's somewhere watching over me, and wherever it is, she's happy.

Hot Cool Summer

BEL MOONEY

Jessie looked out of the window at clouds, and the brilliant blue emptiness above them.

Down below, she thought, people were going about their ordinary lives under grey skies. If they knew, they would surely envy her. Yet she longed to be the same as them. She didn't want this change. How weird, she thought, that you could feel so unlucky, being so lucky. And that dullness could be so desirable. It was such a contradiction, it made her eyes water.

Sitting on the plane, glad the flight attendants had stopped fussing over her – treating her as a kid, because she was on her own – Jessie remembered how she'd been round and round like a fairground ride, swinging this way and that until she felt sick – ever since Mum and Dad told her the news.

"We're going to live in the States," Mum sang out, eyes shining with excitement.

"That was a bit sudden, Liz," Dad protested mildly, looking at Jessie with his earnest, worried look. "I hope you don't mind, Jess."

"Mind? She'll love it!" laughed Mum, dangling her wedge mule from one foot, until it dropped.

"It'll be a big change, hon, but this is the job of my dreams, and I know you'll love Chicago," said Dad.

"But what about my friends? What about school? I won't know... What about...?" Jessie blurted, as that terrible prickling started behind her eyes.

Mum kicked off the other mule and danced around the room, lithe and gorgeous in her tight jeans, tossing her long dark hair. She was trilling an old number, "Chicago! Chicago!" but the door slammed on the line about losing the blues in Chicago as Jessie stormed out. At that moment, she just hated her mother. Banging up the stairs she wailed, "I don't want to move to stupid old America. I'm English!"

Liz Martin had always had a thing about the USA, which Jessie chose not to understand. Mum loved rock 'n' roll, the blues, jukeboxes, cowboy boots, bagels, Hollywood movies, skyscrapers, Navajo turquoise jewellery, American writers. Jessie's dad always joked that she only fell in love with him at college because he came from New York. The funny thing was, Liz said, he was much more like a Brit than the Brits! Nat Martin knew everything about paintings and worked in a big art gallery, organising the exhibitions. He was quiet and gentle, with a liking for tweedy jackets and stripey shirts. As fair as Liz was dark, Nat had pale blue eyes that could see right into Jessie's heart. She looked like him, too. Sometimes, when her parents walked arm in arm down the street, Jessie thought that they looked like a contradiction in terms. Yet they hardly ever fought. "Opposites attract," Mum said.

The flight attendant bent over her. "Is your seatbelt fastened, dear? We're nearly there."

Jessie peered out of the window. Did American clouds look different? Of course not. But this was the new life and she didn't want it. Rosie had cried and cried when she and her parents and two little brothers took Jessie to the airport.

That was the deal she'd made. Rather than leave before the middle of the term and suffer the strangeness of a new American school, she'd insisted they let her finish the school year in England. She could stay in her best friend's wonderful, old, ramshackle house while Mum and Dad found a new home, and chose her new school. Dad had to take up his new post at the Museum of Contemporary Art very quickly, and Mum… well, given the choice between staying and going, she wanted to go. She couldn't wait.

"Dad can't do it all on his own, and I want to start buying and selling as soon as I can." Jessie's mum made good money selling vintage clothes and accessories on the Internet. She'd already collected stuff to take with her.

"Ladies and gentlemen, we are starting our descent to Chicago O'Hare."

"It's only for two years, sweetie – unless we love it, that is."

"I won't love it – I won't!"

Their home, to let, in the hands of an agent. The pain of goodbye, made worse by the look of anticipation on Mum's face. Then those six weeks that were such fun, they made Jessie feel guilty. Rosie's mum was so cosy, so mumsy, and their house was full of the smell of cooking and scented candles. Though Jessie would sometimes cry herself to sleep because she missed her own parents, she still resented them for spoiling the life she knew. Especially Mum. Jessie felt sure that if she hadn't been so keen, Dad would have turned the job down. What was wrong with the one he had? This was going to be so awful…

Bump.

Down to earth. Or rather, American tarmac. Which didn't, after all, look any different from the ground at Heathrow. Then – after all the boring airport stuff, and the airline people treating her like she was nine, or something – there were Mum and Dad waiting in Arrivals, shouting, waving, smiling, hugging.

Jessie was so pleased to see them again, she felt almost shy.

❦ ❦ ❦

Every ten minutes Mum asked, "Do you like it, pet?" and Dad looked worried. The little house they'd found to rent was lovely; her new room was great – but a little red devil got inside Jessie, so that even though she was happy to be a family once more, she wanted it not to be easy. After all, Rosie and the girls had been SO sad, and all the promises of emails and texts didn't alter the fact that this parting might be for good. The thought of a new school, with a whole bunch of American kids, like in all the teen films she'd seen… Well, it made her stomach flip. And the jet lag was starting to kick in.

She felt worse when, after lunch, Dad leaned forward with that anxious look and said, "We've got two things to tell you, hon."

"I can't wait," laughed Mum.

Jessie thought she saw a frown crease her father's brow, but couldn't be sure.

The first bit of news didn't please Jessie one bit. Even though she had just arrived, Dad had to fly off in two days to a museum conference in San Francisco. He had no choice. The new job demanded it.

"Sounds really fun," said Jessie.

"Don't be like that, Jess, it's only for a week," he said softly. "After that, we got all the time in the world."

Yeah, thought Jessie, *time for me to get used to living here and meet a whole lot of strangers who'll laugh at my accent. Great.*

"So," smiled Mum, clutching her hands together in front of her chest as if they contained a wonderful hidden thing, "you and I are going on a trip. A very special one. I want you to see a little bit of the USA right away – and in the best possible way! So… come and see what I've got."

She motioned to Jessie to follow her. Jessie looked at her dad, who gave the faintest of shrugs and nodded at her to obey.

Mum was almost dancing ahead of them, out of the front door, round to the garage, and then she threw up the door with a flourish.

The sun was so hot, Jessie felt sleep settle on her eyelids. All the excitement of arrival had gone already, and whatever Mum had in mind, she was sure of one thing. She didn't want it.

"Look, Jess!' cried Mum, standing back.

Jessie stepped forward. There, in the middle of the empty garage, was a motorcycle. It was silvery-blue with cream panels either side of the petrol tank, which bore the name "Harley-Davidson" in curly black script. The seat was edged with silver studs and there was a studded leather bag on each side. A shaft of sunlight made the chrome sparkle.

'But… whose is it?' asked Jessie.

"Mine!" said her mother, with a funny, childish squeak.

"Dad?"

"It's true, hon. Something Mum's always wanted."

"You never said! Anyway, how can you ride it?"

'Sweetheart, don't you remember I told you I learned when I was a teenager? I got my license then, and loved it, but then… well… you grow up and you stop doing things. When we came here, I told Nat that now I was in the States, I wanted to ride again. So I used all my savings, bought my dream bike, and did a course to bring it all back. Now I feel so confident…"

"Like being a teenager again?" said Jessie. She couldn't keep the sarcastic note out of her voice.

"Sort of," smiled Mum.

"Dad? How could you let her?"

"Aw, Jessie, your mother has to do her thing," said Dad uneasily. "At first, I wasn't sure. But now she's so good at it, and she thought the road trip would be such a great thing for you guys to – "

"Both of us? On that?" shrieked Jessie and took three steps back – as if putting a distance between the mean machine and her would make it go away.

A vision flashed across her mind of Rosie's cuddly mum serving up shepherd's pie in that cosy family kitchen, as the English rain rattled on the window. That was lovely – how things should be. It was where she belonged. Not here.

"Darling, it's going to be wonderful," said Mum, with a new pleading note in her voice. "I've worked it all out. We're riding all the way down to St Louis, and then round – "

"I don't want to!" yelled Jessie, feeling that a river was about to burst its banks behind her eyes. "Why don't you grow up, Mum? It's just so stupid!"

There was a silence.

Jessie's parents stared at each other, and then her dad looked away. In that second Jessie saw her mother's jaw tighten. And she knew that Dad didn't like the plan at all. That they'd quarrelled.

Mum bent to pick something up from the floor behind the bike. It was a silver helmet.

"This is for you," she said flatly. "I thought you'd be excited." Her eyes glistened like the chrome on the Harley. She thrust the helmet into Jessie's hands before walking quickly away.

❦ ❦ ❦

When Jessie woke at last she felt drugged. She tried to work out what time it was back home, then gave up. Back home. But now this was home…

The smell of garlic and barbecued meat made her realise how hungry she felt. The gleaming helmet was on a table on the other side of her beautiful new room, and there was something heavy on the duvet at her feet. She reached down and found a black leather jacket, just her size. It looked worn, as if it had been bought in a nearly-new shop. The leather was slightly scuffed here and there, which just added to the effect. The first word that sprang to her lips as she fingered all the zips was, "Cool!"

But then she remembered, and frowned. The jacket was cool, but she'd look stupid in it, because she wasn't the cool type – not like some of the girls in her old school who hung around, talking about boys non-stop. People would laugh at her. And she didn't want to go riding around on the back of a motorcycle because – now she whispered the truth to herself – the thought terrified her. And in any case, she didn't want the kind of mum who wanted to. It was all just such a bad idea.

When she went downstairs at last, she found her parents out at the back, where smoke from the barbecue drifted up to the mauve and blue sky. The slatted table was set for three. They were sipping white wine and talking quietly.

"Did you like it, sweetheart?" asked Mum, in that

too-bright voice.

Jessie nodded, not trusting herself to speak.

"I bet you look real funky…" Dad began, but Jessie silenced him with a look.

Mum raised her glass, as if in a silent toast. "Let's make a bargain. Let's not mention it again. Tomorrow we'll show you round the city and you can see where Dad works. Then, the day after, I'm going to take him to the airport and when I come back we'll throw a few clothes into plastic bags, put them in the panniers – and just go. OK?"

"Just… go?"

"That's it, hon," Dad chimed in sympathetically. "Best way to do it. And it's your mother's style. Now – let's eat."

🦋 🦋 🦋

Mum was singing about Route 66 at the top of her voice. The blue Harley-Davidson was on the front path, shining in the hot sun. Jessie screwed up her eyes, sweating as she stood there helplessly in jeans and T-shirt, while Mum rushed about, singing the silly song about the road they were going to travel near. "It's an old route," she'd explained. "It'll be fun to find it."

The house was locked up. They were ready. "I'll be too hot in this thick jacket," Jessie moaned, to disguise the fear she felt.

"No, you won't," said Mum, in her briskest voice – as if she, too, had something to hide. "Put it on, zip it up, then put on the gloves and the helmet. Got your sunglasses?"

And that was it. Mum threw her leg over the bike and started the engine. A rumble filled Jessie's ears, as if a grumbling beast had woken from sleep and was now stuttering its complaints. Mum yelled "Get on!" and there was no time to think. The next minute, she was leaning against the little backrest, her hands clutching Mum's waist as they eased out into the street. And panic scrabbled at her heart.

How near the road seemed. The traffic was far too close. A voice in Jessie's head – a thin, small voice drenched in vinegar, an old lady's voice – said, *This shouldn't be happening*. No normal mother would set off with her 13-year-old daughter on a motorcycle. It was too risky. And, even though they were going slowly, carefully, the houses and shops still moved by much too fast. The hot air dried her mouth, as if they were riding into a vast hairdryer.

Jessie closed her eyes tight. When she opened them, she stared straight ahead of her at the back of an anonymous black-and-silver helmet and black leather jacket. Who did they belong to? Some woman who said she was her mother – but who was this stranger? Did she know or care who was behind her – a girl who tensed in terror as they rounded a bend and the bike seemed to tip too far towards the road? What on earth were they doing?

Just then, her mum glanced over her shoulder and yelled, "Isn't this great?"

"Yeah," Jessie shouted back.

They bowled on south, through suburbs, bands of countryside, sprawling strips of small towns – Joliot, Bloomington, Normal. "My mum's not normal," Jessie thought – then found herself grinning at her own little joke, as the wind whipped her cheeks. After a couple of hours, she found herself leaning with the Harley at last, feeling the movement of the road through her own body.

But when they stopped for a sandwich and Mum asked how she was doing, the same old demon put sour words into Jessie's mouth.

"It's so boring."

"What is?"

"Just sitting there. At least in a car you can listen to music, or read."

She was rewarded by the swift dipping of her mother's dark eyes, and that sad little twist at the corner of her mouth.

They sat in silence for a few minutes. Jessie felt cross, guilty and tired. Then, it was as if Liz Martin had come to a decision. She snapped her head up

with a toss of long, dark hair, and a flash of silver
earrings. Leaning back in her seat, she said, "Look
around you, Jess. I mean, look."

"What at?"

"All this. Where we are. In fact – go walk around.
Tell me what you see, OK?"

The mats and menus announced that they were
in "Dixie's Truckers' Home" – a famous Route 66
cafe. It was like being in a time warp. Cheesy old
songs were playing. There was a wonderful smell of
fries and crispy bacon. Jessie wandered about,
looking at the old photos ("Route 66 Hall of
Fame"). The shop sold souvenirs like teddy bears and
little salt-and-pepper sets in the shape of old-
fashioned petrol pumps, mugs and T-shirts with
"Route 66" on them – and so many other funny
things that Jessie found herself thinking, "Rosie
would love all this stuff."

She stopped, surprised. That thought hadn't made
her feel sad, or cross, but – suddenly – lucky. That was
strange.

But still, she was irritated by things like the ladies'
toilet being called "restroom" or "bathroom". How
stupid was that – when you weren't going to have a
rest, and there was no bath? She didn't like people
ordering her to "Have a nice day" or "Enjoy" when
they brought her a drink. All those little things she

enjoyed in American films or television programmes felt weird when she was actually living them. And there was Mum, thinking that, just by putting her on the back of an American motorcycle, she could suddenly be made to feel at home. It was crazy. She'd never belong.

"What do you think?" asked Mum eagerly.

"It's OK – if you like that sort of thing."

"But what's it like?"

Jessie said, "It's just… sort of… American."

"And is that good or bad?"

Jessie didn't reply. How could she? She didn't know.

That night, they stayed in a small motel somewhere on the road, and went out for a Chinese meal. She told Mum all about her time at Rosie's, and Mum asked lots of questions, but nothing could alter the fact that there was a gulf between them. It was symbolised for Jessie by the gleaming motorcycle, which seemed to be taking her away from everything she knew, everything familiar and loved. It had changed her mother into this beautiful woman in black leather who did exactly what she wanted to do, even if nobody else wanted it. Its low rumble was a threat that things would go on changing until Jessie didn't know anything anymore. She was afraid of that road, and where it might lead.

After all, Dad hadn't looked too happy…

As if she could read her mind, Mum asked, "It's OK, isn't it, love? You are having a good time?"

"I don't know why you wanted it, that's all."

"What?"

"The bike. Everything."

"It's hard to explain," said her mum, "it's just that when I'm riding it, I feel… free."

"But you're NOT free! You've got me and Dad."

"No, Jess, I'm not free, and I love my family – but don't you see, sometimes grown-ups have dreams? When I'm on the bike on my own, just riding around, I feel like a different person. And I like that."

Jessie was silent.

"You don't get it, do you?" asked her mum sadly.

Jessie shook her head.

🦋 🦋 🦋

It was hotter than ever, and they rolled south-west, towards St Louis. "There's a week of this," thought Jessie unhappily, as she stared out across fields of maize, and noticed the hideous hoardings that sprouted along the roadside like a crop of weeds.

Just then, there was a low rumble, increasing to a roar, ahead of them in the distance. On the other side of the highway, she saw a cluster of black dots, getting nearer and nearer, closer and closer. Bikers. About ten of them. And as they swept by, each one of them held out his arm in a low salute.

To them.

And her mum did the same, as if she knew the language.

Hey! Jessie thought, *this is like being in a club – a very special, exclusive one.*

"Cool!" she said aloud – to the wind, and the road, and the passing trees, and the back of her mum's helmet.

When they stopped for coffee, a cute teenage boy stopped and examined the Harley. As Mum kicked the stand down, he said, "Nice."

"Thanks," said Mum.

As they strolled towards the diner, Jessie felt herself walking differently – and it wasn't because her bottom was a bit sore from the ride. For the first time since she had left England, she felt really good. She noticed people looking at them, and caught a glimpse of herself in the mirror by the entrance. Blue jeans, white T-shirt, leather jacket with lots of zips, sunglasses and the silver helmet under her arm.

Wow, she thought, *I look great! I look as great as Mum does.*

She felt like a different person.

In the restroom, a couple of young women in their early twenties turned to her enthusiastically.

"Hey – we saw you drive up," one said. "Is that

your mom on the Harley? Wow!"

"Where're you guys going?" asked her friend.

"Down to St Louis, then back up along the river and across to Chicago," Jessie replied, trying to make her voice sound as if she did this every day.

"And you guys are British, too?"

She nodded.

"Man, that's so cool."

Yes, Jessie thought, *it is.*

This time, when she went to sit down, she was grinning broadly. Mum smiled back. "Milkshake?"

"Sure," Jessie said, and leaned back in her chair, hot in the jacket she didn't want to take off. Suddenly it felt like a badge – one she really did want to wear.

As they rolled into the city, Mum was singing a song about St Louis, but her words got lost in the wind, the roar of the engine, and the buzz of traffic. That night they listened to jazz in the open air as the St Louis Arch gleamed in the light from the setting sun. Jessie chewed on ribs, not minding that the sticky sauce coated her cheeks and hands.

"Dad and I drove for miles that year before you were born," Mum said. "We just hired a car and went all the way from Seattle to the Mexican border. It was the most fantastic holiday we ever had."

"Why?"

"Ohh – just being in love, and driving on from

place to place with no plan, and thinking you owned the whole land. It was just the best."

Jessie knew all the stories, but never tired of hearing about when her parents met, what they said, Mum's funny clothes — everything.

"Better than this?" she asked.

"Different," Mum said. "But I'll tell you something — I feel just as young and free as I did then."

"How come?"

"Well, you choose — it's either being on the Harley, or being with my girl."

"Mean girl," Jessie whispered.

"No," Mum said softly, "I asked you to do a hard thing at a hard time. To tell you the truth, love, I was only really thinking about myself, so that was a bit mean of me."

The warm indigo sky wrapped round Jessie like a velvet cloak. A thin silver moon was rising, and on the other side of the road, the waiting motorcycle picked up its soft light. It glimmered at her like the stars, like her mother's smile, like the zips on her jacket. Like the light inside her head.

They lost track of time. Days and nights with the Mississippi river on the right — with Mum telling her about so many things that Jessie thought she'd never learned as much on any school trip. Sometimes the road was horrible, with miles of fast-food places like Wendy's and Taco Bell, and the highway going through everything, and with a pang Jessie found herself remembering the soft green of England.

But then the road would take them to somewhere new, somewhere good. This was now Highway 61, Mum said, and one of her favourite singers, Bob Dylan, had sung about it.

"Cool," Jessie said, although she didn't know whether it was or not. Still, Mum looked pleased. And when the ugliness turned to beauty and then back to ugliness again, Jessie thought how strange it was that you could get to like both – the opposites, the contradictions.

The river was the widest she had ever seen, and sometimes the road was so near it that Jessie could breathe in the smell of water, mud and rich dark earth, and all the lives that had been led along its length: rich people, poor people, slaves. The sun blazed, so they rolled their jackets and fastened them behind Jessie's backrest with bungees. Small motels, the simplicity of unpacking a plastic carrier bag, snuggling together to watch TV, moving on in the morning . . . She began to love the camping feel of it all. And everywhere people talked to them, stared at the bike – and most of all, admired her mother. Her very own biker mum.

At Hannibal, they went on a paddle steamer and rang its bell with a satisfying clang. They visited the pretty house which once belonged to the American writer, Mark Twain. "Oh, this is so GREAT," squealed Mum, with her usual enthusiasm. Jessie had to agree. It was. She told Dad so on the phone, and heard the happiness in his voice.

"And we'll be back together again in a couple of days, hon," he said.

"Unless Mum and I decide to ride on forever and ever!" Jessie joked.

Of course their journey would end. Of course the road would lead them back to Chicago and the new home, new life. Jessie knew that she'd be scared of the new school, and it might be hard to make friends at first, and they might tease her for saying "biscuit" not "cookie", or "pavement" instead of "sidewalk". But how many of the new kids she'd meet would have done something like this? It would be something to tell them. And nothing school could throw at her would be more scary than that first day on the bike, when the road she'd come to love felt like it might eat her up in one bite.

Whatever was going to happen, Jessie lived for now: the squish and squeak of black leather when she and Mum walked arm in arm; leaning her cheek against Mum's back as they rode. Jessie knew she would never be the same again, that all her life she'd remember the Summer of the Road. Moving on. Passing through. With the skies so big over the always-new highway ribboning ahead. And the rumbling, roaring, rolling freedom of it all! Sometimes – remembering, much later – Jessie thought she should really call it the hot cool summer. Just another of life's contradictions.

Mum raised her glass of cola. "Here's to us, love."

"Yeah, and to total mother-daughter cool." Jess grinned, as she clinked her glass against her mother's.

"You know something, sweetheart?" Mum said thoughtfully.

"What's that?"

"You look different – so much older than when we picked you up at O'Hare. Isn't that weird?"

"Must be my smart clothes," smiled Jessie. By now she had nothing clean to wear, and neither did Mum. Their faces were brown, their hair looked terrible, and the hands that reached to touch across the table had the same dirty nails.

Acknowledgements

The publisher would like to thank the copyright holders for permission to reproduce the following copyright material:

"Barn Swallows" copyright © **Amy Boesky** 2006; "Tantie" copyright © **Adèle Geras** 2006; "Missing Out" copyright © **Betty Hicks** 2006; "Mum Never Did Learn to Knock" copyright © **Cathy Hopkins** 2006; "Making It Up" copyright © **Julia Jarman** 2006; "Snow-Globe Moment" copyright © **Shirley Klock** 2006; "The Ninth Dragon" copyright © **Jennifer Kramer** 2006; "The Surprise" copyright © **Jenny Land** 2006; "Hot Cool Summer" copyright © **Bel Mooney** 2006; "Sing" copyright © **Linda Newbery** 2006; "Broken Flower-Heads" copyright © **Kate Petty** 2006; "The Dolphin Bracelet" copyright © **Caroline Pitcher** 2006; "Becoming an MPG" copyright © **Candice Ransom** 2006; "Not Just a Pretty Face" copyright © **Jean Ure** 2006.